LADY CECILIA IS CORDIALLY DISINVITED FOR CHRISTMAS

SECRETS AND SEDUCTION

BOOK 0.5

SHERIDAN JEANE

CONTENTS

Lady Cecilia is Cordially Disinvited for Christmas
Sheridan Jeane

ISBN: 978-1-63303-014-5

Flowers and Fullerton, LLC

Cover Design:
Earthly Charms

Flowers and Fullerton, LLC

*This book is dedicated to my dear friends. You all know who you are.
You've been there for me through some difficult times these past few years,
and your loving support has meant the world to me.
This is for you.*

LADY CECILIA IS CORDIALLY DISINVITED FOR CHRISTMAS

A Secrets and Seduction Book
by
Sheridan Jeane

❀   I   ❀

Devin

December 24, 1850

The train slowed as it approached the station, and the change in its rhythm and motion alerted Devin Montlake to his imminent arrival home. It pulled to a screeching halt as he peered out the window. He was surprised to see his older brother Horace, Viscount Tittle, step out of their family carriage.

On reflection, Horace's presence really shouldn't have come as a surprise. He took his role as heir seriously. Father had drilled family duty into his children from birth. His older sister had fulfilled hers with three children, and Horace, married just six months, would likely announce an heir soon.

Devin had once been held to those same expectations. Now, he was the family's disappointment.

Devin had always tried to be the model son, but pleasing his parents had proven impossible. Their vision for him as a pastor clashed with his need to forge his own path as a barrister, and when he refused, he became their greatest disappointment.

Sacrilege.

He'd always known that standing firm against his parents

would cost him dearly, but the thought of losing their approval still stung. Yet the alternative—living a life dictated by their demands—was unthinkable. Cecilia was worth the sacrifice.

To make matters worse, he also happened to be the only unmarried one of the lot.

Fortunately, he had plans to take steps toward rectifying that omission over the holiday.

He stepped from the train car and onto the platform. The train station reeked of coal smoke, and the frosty air nipped at Devin's skin. He'd need to change into a fresh shirt once he reached his father's estate. His white collar and cuffs had taken on a grayish shade from the soot.

"Devin, you rascal. You made it. Mother had nearly given up on you arriving in time for Christmas." Horace pulled him into a firm hug and then backed away and gave Devin a sharp clap on his back. It was good to know he could always count on his brother.

"I was handed a big case last week, and I needed to prepare. I'd still be in London if not for—" He reconsidered his next words and glanced at his brother. "Lady Cecilia and her family said they'll attend Mother's annual festivities, did they not?"

Horace took a step back and regarded him. "I was under the impression they hadn't been invited this year."

"So I heard. I took matters into my own hands and contacted Lord Babbage to extend an invitation."

The corner of Horace's mouth twitched in a smirk. "Mother is annoyed with you."

"As long as Lady Cecilia comes, I really don't care."

"There was some doubt. Lady Babbage's illness has worsened, and she isn't even feeling up to the mild excitement of a country party, but I was gratified to learn yesterday that Lord Babbage and his daughters decided to attend without her. They plan to return home mid-day on Christmas and will miss the dance."

"I'm relieved to know they're coming, although I'm sorry to hear about Lady Babbage. I must admit, I only came home because I plan to formalize things with Lady Cecilia. I need to speak with her father to finalize our engagement. I hope to set the wedding date for next fall. By then, I'll be firmly established as a barrister. Between her dowry and my income, I should be able to maintain an independent household."

Horace tensed as he absorbed this news. "I didn't realize you'd decided to marry her."

"Of course I'll marry her. That's always been my plan."

"Yes, but I assumed you'd wait until she'd reached the age of eighteen before asking her. You've taken me by surprise." Horace studied him for a moment, his expression unreadable. "You've always been sure about her, haven't you?"

Devin nodded without hesitation. "Always."

Horace's lips pressed into a thin line, but he said nothing more, turning to gaze out the window. The silence spoke volumes.

Devin picked up his valise and gestured toward the waiting carriage. "We should go. No reason to stand here in the cold."

"Yes, let's be off." Horace glanced around and noticed Devin's single piece of luggage. "Just the one bag?"

"I've learned to travel light." Since he'd never bothered to hire a valet after leaving Oxford, keeping things simple had become essential.

Once inside the opulent carriage, Devin plopped his valise by his feet and settled himself against the comfortable cushions. His brother took the seat opposite him, and a moment later the coach lurched forward.

Horace used his boot to shove a heated brick that served as a foot warmer closer to Devin and then stared fixedly out the window. A moment later, he turned his gaze on his brother. "Lord Babbage has had some more bad luck."

Devin's stomach lurched. "Don't tell me he fell for another one of those schemes."

"Perhaps not a scheme, per se, but certainly a risky investment."

Devin sighed heavily. "You'd think he'd have learned his lesson after losing so much money on that train deal a few years back. It nearly ruined him."

"And to lose it all due to a friend's lies. I'm surprised the man ever trusted anyone again after that."

"What happened this time?" Devin asked.

"His newest scheme was based on England's increasing demand for sugar. He noticed a small shortage and rushed to bring in a shipment to market before his competitors. Operated under the banner of some shipping venture—the Mediterranean Mercantile Company, I believe it was called. It might have worked, but unfortunately the ship hit a bad storm, and the cargo was destroyed. I understand he lost a great deal this time. He's said to be nearly destitute."

A chill ran across Devin's shoulders. He let out a sigh. "Why the rush? Why take such a chance? Sugar will still be in demand when the seas are calmer." As a barrister, he'd seen too many cases where a man's desperation made him easy prey—where the eagerness to recover what was lost only led to losing more. Lord Babbage was a good man. Good men were not always careful ones.

Horace cleared his throat. "Lady Cecilia's dowry—"

Devin's gaze snapped to his brother. "Is it gone?"

"I can't say for certain, but I suspect so. Tread carefully. You know how Father can be. He sees catastrophes looming at every turn."

Devin collapsed back against the cushions. That would certainly sabotage his plans for a future with Cecilia. There would be no way for him to purchase a home without her dowry... not where he'd hoped they could live. He knew better than to hope his parents would help. Based on their increasingly frequent demands and their complaints when he wouldn't accede to them, even the minimal support they still provided would soon come to an end.

The countryside beyond the carriage window was stripped bare by winter, the fields dormant and brown, a sharp reminder of the fragility of his plans. He couldn't shake the chill that seeped into his bones—not entirely from the cold.

The remainder of their short drive to the family estate took place in silence. The train station was quite convenient, even if it made the countryside a bit noisier than it had been when he'd been a boy. The estate loomed ahead atop the hill, its stone walls imposing against the pale winter sky.

Once inside, the red-carpeted staircase inside, polished to gleaming perfection, seemed to radiate judgment. Holly garlands adorned the staircase, and the scent of spiced cider lingered in the air. Yet for all its holiday cheer, the house felt suffocating, each perfectly placed ornament a reminder of the expectations bearing down on them.

Devin's mother descended the staircase like a queen surveying her court, her emerald gown catching the light as if to underscore her authority. "Devin, you've finally come home." Her pale hair was swept up in a tight bun. She paused at the last step and peered at his bag with confusion. "But where is your traveling trunk? Don't tell me that's all you brought."

"I can't stay long. I need to leave on Boxing Day."

"Are you trying to break your mother's heart?" his father asked as he swept in from the direction of the library, a book clutched in one beefy hand. "You haven't been home in two years, and now you say you'll only stay two days?" The man's hair had turned a bit grayer, but other than that he was relatively unchanged since Devin's last visit.

"I know. I'm sorry. I have a case I need to argue next week, and it's a complicated one. I should be in London right now preparing for it, but I didn't want to disappoint you." Or Cecilia.

"Hmph." His father's disdain was both loud and obvious.

"That certainly puts a damper on my plans," his mother

complained. "So many of our guests were looking forward to seeing you. Miss Glassford in particular."

"Miss Glassford? I don't recall meeting her." Devin glanced at Horace, who avoided his gaze.

"She's the daughter of a wealthy newcomer to the county," his mother said smoothly. "Such a pleasant young woman. I quite admire her."

Devin suppressed a sigh. A wealthy father. A marriageable daughter. The calculation was obvious. He forced himself not to react. "I look forward to meeting Mr. Glassford and his family." The tight smile he offered should have conveyed all his annoyance, but she chose to ignore it.

"Quite so," his mother said. "I hope you'll make them feel welcome. Miss Glassford is such a pleasant young woman. I quite admire her."

"I'll do what I can. Unfortunately, since my visit is so short, I already won't have much time to devote to Lady Cecilia. I'm hopeful I'll be able to finalize matters with her father."

"You what?" his father interrupted. "What on earth are you babbling on about? What matters? What could you possibly be planning that includes Lord Babbage? The man is a soft-headed imbecile. Don't tell me you're getting yourself involved in one of his schemes."

Devin straightened his spine. "I'm referring to the arrangements I plan to make with Lord Babbage to secure Lady Cecilia's hand in marriage."

His mother let out a soft moan. "Don't tell me that's why you went behind my back and invited them. I thought we'd convinced you of the rashness of that plan. Her family—"

"Her family has had more than its fair share of bad luck. Between Lady Babbage's ill health, the lack of a direct male heir to inherit the title, and Lord Babbage's poorly chosen investments, I'd say they've been extremely unfortunate," Devin said.

"Why would you want to tie yourself to such people?" his

mother asked. "Don't you realize that Cecilia will try to pass them money— *your* money— at every opportunity? And what of your children? That sister of hers is much too precocious. They've let Evangeline run wild. She has no idea how to speak to her betters."

"I've seen it over and over again with horses. Bad breeding makes bad foals," Father intoned.

Devin narrowed his eyes. "Are you suggesting Cecilia is in some way deficient? She's the picture of good health."

"Not of good sense," his mother muttered.

"I think I've heard more than enough." Devin grabbed his valise from where he'd set it on the floor. "I insist you stop criticizing the woman I plan to marry."

His mother's face paled. "Devin, be reasonable. You can't still plan to—"

"I do, Mother. I plan to make Cecilia my wife. You need to accept it."

❧

CECILIA

Cecilia jolted awake when their carriage shook so hard her head bounced against the threadbare backrest.

"Ow," Evangeline shrieked from the seat opposite She shot Cecilia an accusatory glance as she rubbed a spot behind her ear.

"Don't look at me," Cecilia told her sister. "*I* didn't drive the carriage through a rut."

Father let out a faint grunt of agreement without lifting his eyes from his book, *An Illustrated Historical Atlas of the Mediterranean Region*. Was he already hatching some new scheme? She didn't want to know.

Cecilia tucked the wool blanket more tightly around her feet so the heat from the brick foot warmer couldn't escape. She glanced out the window and was disappointed to realize she could only have been dozing for ten minutes at most.

"You look tired," Evangeline said.

Cecilia turned to find her sister staring at her. "I didn't sleep well last night." She leaned her head to one side to stretch her stiff neck.

"Are you nervous about seeing Devin?"

Cecilia shifted on the seat. "More than I care to admit." If not for Devin's unexpected note, she would have slept soundly last night. In it, he said he "needed to speak with her" during the Christmas festivities at his parents' estate.

"You're overthinking it," Evangeline said, her tone matter-of-fact. "If Devin didn't want to marry you, he wouldn't have sent that letter. He's too forthright to waste time with half-measures."

Cecilia gave a wry smile. "And what makes you the expert on Devin's character?"

"I'm observant,' Evangeline replied with a shrug. "You should try it sometime. But if I were you, I'd still be vexed with him," Evangeline said as she leaned comfortably against their father.

"Of course I'm vexed with him. That was his first letter in six months." More than vexed. Unsettled. Couldn't he have been bothered to include some softer words? Perhaps something to reassure her?

"Truly, Cecilia. How dare he send such a cryptic message after remaining silent for so long? If you aren't offended, I'll be offended on your behalf."

The corner of Cecilia's mouth twitched up in a half smile. "I'm offended enough on my own, but thank you."

What did his message mean? Had he returned to break things off? She hadn't seen him in two years. People changed. Had he?

"I bet it's his father's fault," Evangeline said.

"Or his mother's," Father murmured, eyes still on his book. "Devin sent the invitation, not his parents."

Cecilia and Evangeline exchanged glances. Perhaps they should have this conversation when Father wasn't present.

"I'm sure it was nothing more than an oversight." The lie

came easily to Cecilia, but repeating the comments she'd over-heard Lady Vincent say in the village one day would do no one any good. Did Father need to know she'd called him impoverished? Or had described Evangeline as a hoyden? Instead, she held her tongue and turned to gaze out the window at the brown and gray winter landscape.

She couldn't shake her doubts about Devin. Could he have finally fallen under the influence of his parents? He'd never even acknowledged her work at the orphanages—she'd mentioned it in her letters, but his replies, such as they were, had never touched on it. Either he hadn't read them properly, or he simply hadn't thought it worth remarking upon. She wasn't sure which possibility troubled her more.

What if they'd simply grown apart? Two years was a long time.

She shifted her smallest, coldest toe closer to the brick and said nothing.

Devin might just as easily want to meet with her so they could move forward with an engagement. It had never been put into words, but he'd broadly hinted that this was what he wanted. It had been what she had wanted too—once, without reservation. Now she found herself wondering if wanting something was the same as being certain of it.

She pulled her hand from her rabbit-fur muff and slipped it inside her cloak to check her pocket. Yes, the small box containing Devin's gift was still there, exactly as it should be.

"What are you doing?" Evangeline asked.

"Nothing."

"Don't be ridiculous. I can see you're doing *something*— oh, of course. You're nervous about Devin's gift. Is it because the woman is so scantily clad?"

Cecilia snatched her hand from her pocket and stuffed it back into her fur muff. "Now you're the one being ridiculous. She's wearing Roman robes, which were quite appropriate for the time."

"But are they appropriate for a barrister?"

"It's a perfectly appropriate gift," Father said.

"I'm not suggesting *he* wear Roman robes," Cecilia said. "Please, Evangeline. Stop pestering me." Was her sister in the right? Had she chosen poorly with this gift? She always worried about doing the right thing when she was with Devin and his family. He could be terribly straitlaced at times, but his parents were even worse. Lady Vincent clearly believed Mother's illness was due to a weakness of character. She was forever telling Mother that she simply needed to put it out of her mind and try harder if she wanted to get better. As if consumption were nothing more than a cold.

Lord Vincent was just as bad. After Father had been bilked in that railway development fiasco a number of years ago, Lord Vincent had crowed to anyone who would listen, bragging that he hadn't invested in it as well. He conveniently left out the fact that he'd only backed out of the deal at the last minute due to a lack of funds.

Cecilia's family certainly had more than its share of bad luck. Cecilia and Evangeline had no other siblings, and with no son to inherit, their father's estate would go to an estranged cousin. It was unlikely he'd be willing to financially support Father's widow and children, so it was essential that Cecilia marry well. Of course, Father was in excellent health, but if their bad luck continued, something was certain to happen to him.

Cecilia glanced at her father, his worn features illuminated by the dim carriage light. His schemes, his failures—they weighed on her, even when she tried to push them aside. Could she really leave it all behind for a new life with Devin? Or would she be tethered to her family's troubles forever?

She pushed her worries away. It was ridiculous to borrow trouble.

"Do you think Mr. Montlake will ask you to marry him?" Evangeline asked.

Cecilia tensed and then frowned at her sister. "I think you ask too many questions."

Evangeline rolled her eyes in that way only a younger sister could.

Cecilia shot her a quelling glare.

Evangeline stuck out her tongue.

Cecilia found herself rolling her eyes too. In disdain.

"Will he?" Evangeline insisted.

"How should I know? Do I read minds?" Would he? Did she even want him to? What would she say if he did? Or worse, what if he didn't?

The thought of Devin breaking things off with her hit her like a blow to the stomach. The idea that he might not care for her as much as she did for him left her shaken.

She needed to prepare herself for that eventuality because his silence could certainly be taken as evidence of his waning interest. And if it wasn't? Then he surely needed to provide her with an excellent excuse for not contacting her.

Did such an explanation even exist?

As the carriage turned, Lord and Lady Vincent's estate loomed on the hilltop. In the next two days, her future would be decided.

2

Cecilia

The moment the carriage stopped, Cecilia fought the urge to run inside and find Devin. The suspense gnawed at her. She needed answers.

Lord Babbage exited first, and Evangeline darted out after him, ignoring his outstretched hand. Cecilia longed to do the same but forced herself to accept her father's assistance with a decorous nod. At seventeen, she had to appear every bit the suitable fiancée—no childish antics allowed.

Evangeline delicately shook mud from her foot. Somehow, she'd managed to step into the lone puddle next to the walkway leading to the front door.

Cecilia took her father's arm as her sister scampered toward the front door ahead of them. Being a responsible adult had its drawbacks at moments like these. All she wanted to do was run inside that house, track down Devin, and cajole him into proposing right away.

Instead, she behaved like a proper lady.

"I wish your mother could be here," Cecilia's father said. "She always makes these visits go more smoothly."

Cecilia patted his hand. "We'll be fine. It's only for one day."

He let out a heavy sigh. "I'm sure you're right."

Evangeline located the bristled boot cleaner by the front door and slid her foot through the device, brushing the dirt and mud from her shoe. By the time Cecilia and her father joined her, it was clean enough to allow her to enter the house without making a mess.

The butler opened the door, his expression as impassive as the polished wood-paneled walls within. The house, with its sharp chill and formal decor, seemed to welcome guests grudgingly. Cecilia handed over her cloak, the muffled hum of voices from the drawing room prickling her nerves.

Devin's familiar laugh drifted toward her, a low, cultured sound that warmed her chest. She followed the noise to the stately drawing room, its blue-upholstered furniture striking a cold contrast against the dark panels. The room, like Lady Vincent herself, exuded elegance and detachment—beautiful but uninviting.

Evangeline immediately began to move toward the source of the festive noises, but Father stopped her with a heavy hand on her shoulder. "You need to freshen up first. I believe your footwear could use some attention."

Cecilia glanced down and noticed the wet stains on Evangeline's shoe and the hem of her skirt. Fortunately, her own clothing was immaculate. "I think I'll let Lady Vincent know we're here before I go to our room," she said.

Father nodded as he firmly redirected his younger daughter toward the staircase. "We'll see you shortly."

As they headed upstairs, Cecilia followed the sound of voices into Lady Vincent's cold and stately drawing room. The furniture was upholstered in a wintery shade of blue that Cecilia always found off-putting and incongruous in the dark, wood-paneled space.

Devin stood out from the crowd. His height and bearing

always made it easy for her to spot him. Two years. She had not laid eyes on him in two years, and her first sight of him was this — his attention given freely and easily to a woman she had never met.

He was currently chatting with an elegantly dressed, petite young woman Cecilia didn't recognize. She glanced down at her own traveling gown and wondered briefly if she'd made a mistake by not changing first.

She had to accept it. Devin could do much better than to marry her— he could be with someone like the woman he was talking to. She was clearly someone of means.

She'd believed he'd spot her the moment she walked into the room, but that had been a fantasy. An infantile delusion born from reading too many novels.

Movement caught her eye, and she spotted Lady Vincent beckoning her. The woman wore an impatient expression, so Cecilia assumed she'd been trying to catch her attention for some time.

Since her stated intention was to let Lady Vincent know they'd arrived, she should probably face the harridan.

"Lady Cecilia, you and your family have arrived," Lady Vincent said, her tone clipped, her expression pinched. She gestured to the petite woman beside her. "Allow me to introduce Lady Judith Glassford."

"It's lovely to meet you, Lady Cecilia. We're new to the area, and we haven't had the opportunity to meet many people yet."

Lady Judith. Not Lady Glassford—which meant the title was hers by birth, not by marriage. Cecilia glanced at Mr. Glassford across the room, with his new-money confidence and his too-fine coat, and understood a little better the quality of Lady Judith's smile.

"You must be the family that purchased the Bertram estate," Cecilia said.

"Quite so. We find it to be most charming."

"Our estate isn't far from yours," Cecilia said.

"In that case, you must meet my daughter, Miss Glassford. I don't want to interrupt her conversation with Mr. Montlake, though. He's such a learned man, don't you think? Quite refined."

Cecilia blinked. A woman who had married down would naturally want her daughter to marry up. The mathematics of it were quite predictable—as was the fawning remark about Devin. "Very much so."

"Lady Cecilia has known our son since she was in leading strings. She and our daughter Belinda were the closest of companions in their youth."

That caught Cecilia off guard. "Were we?"

Lady Vincent shot her a quelling gaze.

Cecilia coughed. "Of course. Bosom friends," she lied. Lady Vincent was explaining Cecilia's intimacy for Lady Judith's benefit —establishing her as practically family, and therefore no romantic threat. How reassuring for them. She cast about for a plausible detail. "She was quite kind to me when I fell and skinned my knee. Has she arrived yet? I should so like to catch up with her."

Lady Vincent's expression softened briefly—the first genuine emotion Cecilia had seen from her since arriving. "She is reaching the end of her confinement and can't travel now, but we hope to see her here next year."

"She already has two children, does she not?" Lady Judith asked. "How lovely for you when your grandchildren come to visit you." She squeezed Lady Vincent's hand as she eyed her daughter. "Mr. Glassford and I cherish the hope of becoming grandparents someday. Perhaps we can one day share that joy with you."

Share. An odd word choice, unless one imagined a future in which the joy was literally shared—the same grandchildren belonging to both families.

"Is your daughter betrothed?" Cecilia asked.

Evangeline materialized at her elbow—shoe evidently cleaned to satisfaction—and slipped her hand into Cecilia's. Lady Vincent's gaze flicked to her briefly with the particular expression she reserved for children and inconveniences, then returned to Lady Judith without a word of acknowledgment.

Evangeline didn't appear to notice. Or perhaps she simply didn't mind.

"Oh, my, no," Lady Judith said, waving the words away as though embarrassed. "I'm just a hopeful mother."

Lady Vincent stared at Devin, as did Lady Judith. A moment later, the two women shared a conspiratorial glance.

So. *That* was what this was.

A movement on the other side of the room drew her eye before she could dwell on it. Mr. Glassford stood near the window, a glass in hand, his gaze fixed not on his wife or daughter but on Cecilia's father, who had just entered the room. It was too steady for idle social observation. Too deliberate.

Curious.

She ignored the matchmaking pair a moment longer and risked a glance at Devin. Her chest tightened. That smile—easy, unguarded—was not the smile of a man being politely attentive. It was the smile of a man who was genuinely pleased.

She had spent months wondering whether his silence meant indifference. Now she rather wished she didn't know.

"If you'll excuse me, my sister has arrived. I need to speak to her."

She moved toward the door with more purpose than grace. Devin looked up as she passed—their eyes met briefly—and she looked away first. She could feel her composure beginning to fray at the edges and she had no intention of letting it go entirely in Lady Vincent's drawing room.

At the door she found Evangeline, whose expression of exasperation suggested someone was about to be taken to task.

"They've gone too far this time," Evangeline began.

"Not now," Cecilia said, her voice lower than she intended. "Please."

Evangeline read her face in an instant. She glanced toward Devin, already moving toward them, and stepped deliberately into his path. "Go," she said quietly. "I'll handle this."

Cecilia went. At the door, she glanced back. Lady Vincent's hand was on Devin's arm, drawing him away, intentionally preventing him from following her. Evangeline stood her ground between them, expression serene.

She had held herself together this long. She could manage the stairs.

She turned and fled to the next floor. Reaching their familiar room, the one they'd been given every year since she'd been a young girl, she shoved open the door—only to freeze.

A man she didn't recognize sat in the chair by the window, his expression equally startled.

She barely stifled a scream.

"What's the meaning of this?" The man blustered as he bolted out of his chair.

"I— I..." Cecilia peered around the room. It looked exactly the same as it had the last time she'd stayed here.

"Cecilia," Evangeline said from behind her. "We haven't been given this room this year. Apparently, when Father told Lady Vincent that Mother wasn't coming, she assumed none of us would be here and gave our regular room to Mr. Glassford and his family."

"I do beg your pardon, Mr. Glassford," Cecilia said.

He let out an irritated huff of disapproval. "How awkward. Apparently, we've displaced you. My apologies." He stiffly bowed his head.

More than you can possibly know, Mr. Glassford. "Not at all. Please excuse us."

She paused for just a moment in the doorway—their usual room, and she knew it well. The writing desk beneath the window. A traveling case on the table beside it. The small chair angled toward the fire. Everything exactly as she remembered, and none of it hers anymore.

She pulled the door shut and followed Evangeline down the corridor.

✺ 3 ✺

Cecilia

Cecilia surveyed the bedchamber they'd been assigned. The small room was a far cry from the one she and Evangeline usually shared, with its spacious armoire and grand views. Here, even the wardrobe felt cramped, with lace spilling out as if the gowns themselves were trying to escape confinement.

"We've been demoted," Cecilia said, striding to the wardrobe. She yanked the door open and tugged at her pink gown for the day. It was wedged so tightly that when she finally freed it, two more dresses tumbled to the floor. Huffing, she tossed the pink gown onto the bed and shoved the fallen dresses back inside before slamming the door shut.

She should have stuck to her plan. If she'd changed before seeing Devin, maybe she wouldn't have felt so inadequate standing there in her travel-worn dress while Miss Glassford dazzled him in her modish finery. Not that it would have mattered—Miss Glassford was perfection.

"That isn't a surprise," Evangeline said, watching her sister's movements with raised brows. "Lady Vincent always finds fault with everyone in our family. Why you'd want to marry her son, I'll never understand." She paused, her eyes widening. "Not that I don't like Devin. He's perfectly nice. It's just his mother—" She shuddered dramatically.

"I believe she's found someone she prefers as a bride for him," Cecilia replied, her voice clipped.

"No!" Evangeline's indignation was immediate.

"Yes. And her parents are staying in our usual room," Cecilia said, grabbing the pink gown and smoothing the fabric with precise, almost mechanical motions.

Evangeline let out a tut of annoyance and took over, deftly arranging the voluminous skirt. "You know how devious Lady Vincent can be. Don't let her get to you."

Cecilia fumed as she unbuttoned her dark-gray traveling dress and shrugged it off her shoulders. She untied the bow holding the skirt in place, but the heavy petticoats beneath kept it from falling to the floor. With a sharp tug, she pulled the skirt over her head, muttering, "You wouldn't be so blasé if you'd been the one introduced to the mother of your replacement."

Evangeline stilled, her gaze narrowing. "Replacement? What are you talking about?"

"Lady Judith Glassford," Cecilia said, her voice muffled as she wrestled with the skirt. "Wife of Mr. Glassford." She tossed the heavy fabric onto the bed with a frustrated huff.

Evangeline quickly retrieved it, hanging it neatly in the wardrobe as Cecilia would have tossed it aside again. "Lady Vincent certainly knows how to irritate you."

"She introduced me to the woman, then practically paraded her daughter in front of Devin," Cecilia said, staring at the lovely pink confection she'd chosen for today. Its high neckline and V-shaped collar had once felt like the perfect choice—Devin had even once commented on how lovely her throat was. But now, she wasn't sure why she'd bothered.

"He didn't even notice me," she whispered.

"You know what you need to do," Evangeline said firmly.

Cecilia hesitated, her heart sinking. "What's the point? Devin didn't even notice me. And his mother—"

"Is a menace," Evangeline interrupted. "Which is why you need to show her you're not afraid of her schemes. Don't let her win, Cecilia."

Cecilia took a breath, willing her shoulders to steady. "You're right."

"Of course I am," Evangeline said with a wink. "Now let's get you ready for battle."

Evangeline picked up the pink gown and held it out, ready for Cecilia to step into it without mussing her hair. In moments, the bodice was laced, and Cecilia stood before the mirror, her reflection almost unfamiliar in its determined resolve.

"How do I look?" Cecilia asked.

"Like you're about to take that Glassford woman down a notch—or ten."

"Perfect."

Evangeline caught her arm before she could reach the door.

"Wait." Her voice dropped. "Before we go down—there's something I need to tell you."

Cecilia turned. Something in her sister's expression stopped her from reaching for the handle.

"After you left the drawing room," Evangeline said, "I followed the Glassfords. They slipped out just after you did—I don't think they wanted to be caught up in the scene with Devin. I stayed close behind them on the stair. They didn't hear me."

Cecilia waited.

"He said Papa's name. And then he said something about a shipping company. The Mediterranean Mercantile Company." Evangeline watched her sister's face. "I recognized it because I heard Papa mention it—the name he always says like a curse word, when he thinks no one can hear him.

The Mediterranean Mercantile Company.

The cold that moved through Cecilia had nothing to do with the draughty corridor.

"Lady Glassford said something about the timing having been fortunate." Evangeline's jaw tightened. "And he laughed. A quiet sort of laugh—like a man who is very pleased with himself and doesn't need anyone else to know it." She paused. "And then he said, Babbage never suspected. Those words exactly. I'm certain of it."

The noise of the house went on around them—children somewhere overhead, the distant clink of cutlery being laid in the dining room, a burst of laughter from the drawing room. Everything ordinary. Everything unchanged.

"I don't know precisely what it means," Evangeline said. "The business of it escapes me. But I know it isn't good."

"You're right," Cecilia said. "It isn't."

She understood it too clearly. *Babbage never suspected.* The Mediterranean Mercantile Company had taken her father's money—his investment in a shipment of sugar, the gamble that was supposed to restore their fortunes. The loss that was behind the economies they'd been making all year, the staff quietly let go, the house that had gone cold this winter because coal was expensive, the careful silences at table when the subject of money came too close.

And Mr. Glassford had found it *fortunate.*

She became aware that her hands were cold. She pressed them flat against her skirts.

"You did right to tell me," she said. "Don't mention this to Papa. Not right now. It will only upset him...and Mother."

For a moment Evangeline said nothing. The mention of their mother did that—settled over both of them like a change in the weather, quieting everything else. Then she looked at Cecilia steadily—that old look, the one that too often made Cecilia feel she was the younger of the two. "What are you going to do?"

"I don't know yet." It wasn't quite a lie. She didn't know the shape of it yet. But something had already settled in her chest, quiet and purposeful, like a decision forming before she'd consciously made it. "I need to think."

Evangeline nodded once, accepting this. She knew better than to push.

Noisy feet pounded down the corridor outside their bedroom door. Either a pack of wild dogs had invaded the house, or an excited group of children had been promised sweets.

Cecilia took a deep breath, opened the door, and sailed out into the hallway with her sister following behind. Ahead of her, a pack of children disappeared down the staircase. That was one nice thing about Lord and Lady Vincent's Christmas house party — there were always lots of children around, and they were encouraged to take part in nearly all of the festivities.

"Let's head back to the drawing room," Cecilia said as she led the way down the staircase.

"Do you mind if we stop in the library first? I'd like to borrow something to read while we're here. Lord Vincent has all of Mr. Dickens's books. I'm dying to read more of *David Copperfield.*"

"Let's do that first so we don't forget."

When they reached the foyer, the front door burst open as two men in snow-dusted overcoats hauled in a large, freshly cut pine tree. After a moment, Cecilia recognized one of the men as being Devin's older brother, Horace Montlake, Lord Tittle.

"Lady Cecilia, Lady Evangeline," Horace greeted with a polite tilt of his head as he hefted the large pine tree into the foyer.

"Good day, Lord Tittle," Cecilia replied, distracted by the looming confrontation with Devin. The scent of pine and the bustle of servants felt surreal, like a backdrop to the storm raging in her chest.

"I'll leave you to your endeavors," Cecilia said. "Good day, Lord Tittle."

As they reached the door leading to the library, Cecilia heard a man's voice from within. She paused to listen briefly, not wanting to interrupt.

"From what I gather," the man said, "he invested in a shipment of sugar."

Cecilia knew that voice. It was Lord Vincent, Devin's father.

"The ship was caught in a storm, and the cargo was ruined. Sugar doesn't like saltwater," Lord Vincent said, his voice dripping with disdain.

Cecilia froze, the words cutting through her like shards of ice.

"That family has the worst luck imaginable," he continued. "Perhaps it's a curse. I can't think of another explanation for how Babbage consistently fails."

She stumbled back, the world tilting as the weight of his disdain crashed over her. Her father. Her family. Reduced to nothing more than a joke.

She glanced at Evangeline to see her sister's eyes wide with dismay. "We should leave."

"I agree." Evangeline scowled. "I don't really want to borrow one of *his* books anymore."

Lord Vincent was still speaking as Cecilia backed away, but thankfully she couldn't make out his words. She didn't think she could bear to hear more spiteful things come out of the man's mouth.

A moment later, a different voice rose inside the room. An angry one. It only took Cecilia a moment to place it, but she had no doubt to whom it belonged.

Devin.

It had taken her a little longer to recognize it because she'd rarely heard it raised in anger.

"Father, you know where I stand," he said. "You know why I'm here. That hasn't changed. You don't need to keep listing your reasons why Cecilia and I make a bad match. I'm perfectly aware of them."

She stumbled and let out a gasp. If he'd slapped her, it couldn't have shocked her more. She wouldn't have believed it if she hadn't heard the words from his own lips.

Devin thinks they'd make a bad match?

Before she could recover from the shock, a figure appeared in the doorway. Devin, his expression thunderous, charged through it and plowed directly into Cecilia.

She stumbled into him, her breath caught between fury and despair.

"I assure you, Mr. Montlake, I don't need your defense or your pity," she said, her voice trembling. "And I certainly don't need to marry a man who thinks we'd make a bad match."

"Cecilia, that's not what I—"

"Don't," she said sharply, her eyes blazing. "You've made yourself perfectly clear. And now I'll do the same—I wouldn't marry you if you were the last man alive."

Devin opened his mouth, but nothing came out. Had she given him such a set-down that he'd become speechless? She hoped this didn't happen to him often. As a barrister who regularly argued cases in court, words were his tools. If just anyone could render him speechless, he wouldn't be very good at his job.

Cecilia didn't wait for him to regain his voice. She spun on her heel and headed directly for the staircase. It was only at that moment that she realized what she'd just done.

I've broken things off with him.

Quite definitively.

Her stomach tightened. She forced herself to inhale and keep moving.

Had she just made the worst mistake of her life?

She placed her hand on the newel post and glanced back. Evangeline had positioned herself firmly between Cecilia and Devin, one hand on his forearm, talking steadily. Devin wasn't listening—all his attention was fixed on Cecilia, his expression shifting through something she couldn't read.

She didn't wait to find out what it was.

She climbed the stairs without looking back again.

❈   4   ❈

Devin

Devin stood in the hallway, helpless, as Cecilia fled up the staircase. Each step she took away from him cut deeper into his chest.

"The least you can do is refrain from chasing her down," Evangeline said, gripping his forearm with surprising strength. "Can't you see how upset she is? She'd hate to make a scene."

"She misunderstood," Devin said, his voice tight. "I need to explain—"

"Of course you do. But not now." Evangeline's gaze was unyielding. "You've already upset her enough. Let her calm down."

He exhaled heavily, his eyes fixed on the staircase. "I didn't mean for any of this to happen."

"Didn't you?" Evangeline's tone sharpened. "You're terrible at writing letters, Devin. Don't you realize how that makes her feel? Like she doesn't matter. Like she's not even part of your life."

"I've been working nonstop," he argued, his frustration spilling over. "I wake up before dawn, come home after dark, and collapse into bed. I didn't think—"

"Exactly. You didn't think," she interrupted. "A few lines to show her you cared—was that really too much to ask?"

Devin clenched his jaw, guilt gnawing at him. He hadn't written because every word felt inadequate. Writing only made him miss her more, but now he saw the damage his silence had done. He opened his mouth to respond, but before he could speak, Lady Elizabeth appeared around the corner.

"Evangeline!" Elizabeth beamed, her dark curls escaping their bun. "You're here! When did you arrive?"

"Not long ago," Evangeline said, her voice softening. She returned her friend's embrace.

"I assume that means Cecilia is here as well. How splendid!" Her lively eyes seemed to dance with excitement. "You must come with me to the kitchen. Catherine told me that Cook just pulled fresh gingerbread from the oven, and I'm going there straightaway to wheedle a piece from her." One of the riotous black curls Elizabeth tried to tame with a sedate bun suddenly popped lose and fell into her eye. She swiftly tucked it behind one ear.

"Catherine's here too?" Evangeline asked.

"She went to find her brother and tell him about the gingerbread. Hurry, before word spreads and it's all gone." She grabbed hold of Evangeline's hand and started drawing her toward the back of the house.

Horace's voice cut through the hallway. "What's all this commotion about?"

"Fresh gingerbread," Elizabeth said with a grin. "And clotted cream. You're coming, aren't you, Lord Tittle?"

Horace chuckled. "I might."

Devin barely registered their conversation. His attention lingered on the empty staircase. Should he go after Cecilia now? Apologize? Explain?

Horace clapped a hand on Devin's shoulder. "Come with me. I need your keen eye at the stone mill. The horses are ready."

Devin hesitated, glancing again at the staircase. He needed to give Cecilia time, didn't he? With a resigned nod, he followed his brother.

* * *

Ten minutes later, Devin and Horace rode along the muddy, frozen path toward the old stone mill. The river's murmuring grew louder as they neared, mingling with the crunch of hooves breaking through the semi-frozen ground. Yet Devin barely noticed. His thoughts were fixed on Cecilia.

"You've been quiet," Horace said, his tone probing. "Something wrong?"

Devin sighed, debating how much to share. "Father ambushed me in the library earlier, lecturing me about how unsuitable Cecilia is. I lost my temper. Cecilia overheard just enough to think I agreed with him."

Horace winced. "What did she say?"

"She told me she wouldn't marry me if I were the last man alive." The words replayed in his mind, each syllable a fresh sting.

The stone mill emerged from the trees, its pale gray walls softened by the fading light. Horace dismounted first, gesturing for Devin to follow. "That's quite the mess. Do you want her back?"

Devin slid from his horse, tying the reins to a low fence near the mill. The question hit harder than he expected, settling like a weight in his chest. Did he want her back? Yes. The answer was painfully clear.

"Maybe I'm not the right man for her," he admitted quietly, staring into the mill's shadowed doorway. "Her father's an earl. She could marry a nobleman instead of a younger son with no title."

Horace retrieved a lantern from the doorway, lighting it with practiced efficiency. The warm glow illuminated the dusty space, revealing stacked crates and a table pushed against one wall. "Devin, don't be ridiculous. Cecilia's never cared about titles. What matters to her are deeds. And, despite everything, she loves you. The real question is, do you love her enough to fight for her?"

Devin's chest tightened. How could he let her go?

Horace set the lantern on the table, its light casting shifting shadows. "Wait here. I need to check the new steel cogs for the mill. Won't take a minute." He disappeared into the back room, his footsteps echoing.

Devin leaned against the doorframe, staring into the dim interior. Was he selfish to want Cecilia for himself? Would she be better off with someone who wrote letters, communicated clearly, and didn't take her for granted? Someone whose family would embrace her instead of pushing her away?

Horace returned, brushing his hands on his coat. "The work's coming along well. But you're still brooding."

Devin straightened. "Maybe she could do better than me."

"Better?" Horace barked a laugh. "Devin, she doesn't want 'better.' She wants you. Remember the time one of their gardeners accidentally killed that rabbit with his scythe? Cecilia was beside herself when she found out the doe was nursing. She tracked down the kits, fed them goat's milk every four hours, and raised them until they could fend for themselves."

Devin's lips quirked at the memory. "And 'fend' they did. Her family's gardener was ready to tear his hair out when those rabbits started raiding the kitchen garden. She wouldn't let him harm a single one. It drove the poor man mad."

Horace chuckled, his eyes gleaming. "Or when she gave away her old clothes without realizing her nurse relied on selling them for extra money. The woman nearly quit on the spot."

"She said the nurse's priorities were wrong," Devin added, a genuine smile breaking through. "That money wasn't as important as helping people in need."

"That's the woman you fell in love with," Horace said, clapping a hand on Devin's shoulder. "She's always known who she is. The question is, do you?"

Devin stared at his brother, the truth crystallizing. "That's the woman I love. And I've taken her for granted. I need to show her how much she means to me."

Horace grinned. "Then stop brooding and go fix it. I'll find some excuse to keep Mother occupied."

❦   5   ❦

Cecilia

After searching in vain for her father, Cecilia finally returned to her bedchamber. Moments later, he entered, carrying a plate of gingerbread slathered with clotted cream.

"For you, my dear," he said, handing her the plate. "Evangeline said she thought you'd be up here."

"Thank you." She stared at the food. Even the heavenly scent of Cook's famous gingerbread couldn't pull her from her despair. It wasn't as if she were two and everything could be mended with a treat and a kiss. Some problems were too big for such simple comforts. "I need to talk to you."

"Evangeline said that too." He sat heavily in the chair beside her. "What's troubling you, Cecilia? You look devastated."

She hesitated, unsure how to begin. "I overheard some things today that I found rather hurtful. I wasn't sure if I should tell you, but I decided it's best if you know."

His brow furrowed deeply. "What did you hear?"

"Lord Vincent was talking about our family's bad luck."

Father let out a weary sigh. "I've spoken to him before about his habit of spreading gossip. He'll refrain for a while, but then he forgets. I'll have to remind him again."

"It wasn't just gossip this time. He said we're cursed." Her voice cracked. "You know how people can be. If that kind of story spreads..."

Her father paled. "I feared that rumor might surface someday. Some people are so superstitious." His voice grew quieter. "This could make things even harder for us."

Cecilia held her breath, her chest tightening. Finally, she released it in a rush. "Devin told him he's perfectly aware of why we make a bad match."

Her father's expression froze. "He what?"

"Don't make me repeat it."

His jaw tightened, bitterness creeping into his tone. "I expected better of him, but I should have known. The apple doesn't fall far from the tree."

She bit her lip. Devin had always seemed different from his parents—generous where they were grasping, principled where they were selfish. But perhaps he was like them in ways she hadn't seen before. His rigid adherence to rules, his inability to navigate the gray areas of life... Was that how he saw her? As a mistake to avoid?

Her pain sharpened. Maybe she'd been right to break things off. If he couldn't value her enough to communicate or fight for her, what future could they have?

"Sometimes love isn't enough," she said softly. "There has to be trust, respect, and openness. Without those, the relationship will crumble."

Her father's face softened. "I— I broke things off with Devin," she confessed, her voice trembling.

Her father sat back abruptly, his brow lifting in surprise. "You broke things off?"

"Yes," Cecilia said, her voice trembling as she avoided his gaze.

To her astonishment, a slow, wry smile crept across his face.

He leaned forward, resting his forearms on his knees, and let out a low chuckle. "Well, I can't say I'm heartbroken."

She blinked. "You're... not upset?"

He shook his head, the smile still lingering. "I've never told you this, but Lady Vincent and I have a long-standing... shall we say, incompatibility."

"What do you mean?"

"Oh, it goes back years. Let's just say your mother and I endured one too many of her social slights before we finally stopped trying to maintain the friendship. She's a woman who values her status above all else, and I've no doubt she passed that trait on to her son."

Cecilia stiffened. "Devin isn't like that."

"No?" He arched a skeptical brow. "Perhaps not entirely. But I've watched him, Cecilia. He's rigid, like his father. A rule-follower through and through. And a man who can't adapt... well, he'll find it hard to make a marriage work with someone as spirited as you."

Her chest tightened. "You really believe that?"

He hesitated, his gaze softening. "I know you're hurting now, but yes, I do. I've always wanted a better match for you. Someone who sees your fire and admires it, not someone who tries to douse it. And if I never have to share a dinner table with Lady Vincent, I'll consider that a win."

A startled laugh burst from her. "Papa!"

He smiled at her reaction, though his expression quickly turned serious. "But don't mistake me, Cecilia. I'm sorry for your pain. It's clear how much you cared for him."

She wiped her eyes, her emotions tangled in a confusing knot. "It hurts, Papa."

He leaned forward, taking her hand in his. "I know it does, my dear. Hearts heal in time, though. And you'll find someone who deserves you. Someone who values all of you—not just the parts that fit their plans."

❧ 6 ☙

Devin

Devin wiped his boots before stepping inside, the warmth of the house doing little to ease his tension. A footman appeared promptly, taking his coat and hat as Horace disappeared down the hall.

Devin wasted no time. He followed the sound of laughter toward the salon, where the chatter of guests mingled with the festive scents of cinnamon, cloves, and pine.

The room was alive with Christmas preparations. Guests sat at tables covered in paper, ribbons, and baubles. Large wooden storage boxes, their lids thrown open, revealed Mother's growing collection of ornaments, a hobby she had embraced with uncharacteristic enthusiasm thanks to Queen Victoria's love of Christmas.

He spotted Cecilia instantly. She sat among a group of women, deftly crafting paper cornucopias filled with nuts and dried fruit. Her soft pink gown highlighted her graceful form, and the delicate V-shaped collar drew his eye. The sight of her sent a pang through his chest.

Nearby, Mother sat beside Miss Glassford, tying bundles of

cinnamon sticks with ribbon. Children pressed cloves into oranges, their giggles punctuating the hum of activity. The scene was so idyllic it might have been pulled from one of Mother's prized holiday books.

Devin couldn't afford to linger. He summoned a footman and gave him a message for Cecilia, then retreated to the library to wait.

The library was quieter but still carried the holiday's presence. Bowls of potpourri filled the room with pungent holiday scents, nearly overwhelming the comforting smell of paper and leather bindings. He paced, rehearsing what he would say.

The door creaked open, and Cecilia entered, holding one of the paper cones. Her eyes met his, and her expression immediately darkened.

"I'm looking for Evangeline," she said, her voice clipped. "She sent a message asking me to meet her here." She scanned the room, clearly searching for her sister.

Devin stepped forward. "I sent the message. I needed to speak with you, and I didn't want anyone to know you were meeting me here."

Her lips thinned, and her grip on the paper cone tightened. Without a word, she turned to leave.

"Please, Cecilia," he said, his voice raw. "Don't go. I know you're angry with me, but if I ever meant anything to you, stay and hear me out."

She stopped in the doorway, then turned slowly. Her gaze was steely. "There's no need. You've made your feelings toward me perfectly clear. I've already told my father that we're through. There's nothing left to say."

Her words hit like a blow, but he refused to flinch.

"I'm sorry I didn't write to you and took you for granted."

She frowned. Not the response he was hoping for, but perhaps the one he most deserved. Then, she took a single step toward him. "Why? Answer me that. Why didn't you write to me? How could you simply stop communicating with me?" Her voice cracked, the pain in it undeniable. "How could you just... disappear?" She looked down, her tone dropping. "I even imagined that you'd found someone else."

"Someone else? Never." He shook his head. "I thought you understood how busy I was. I told you I was working hard to establish myself as a barrister."

Her voice sharpened. "A few lines, Devin. That's all it would have taken to let me know you cared. Instead, you left me in the dark, imagining the worst."

"There's never been anyone else, Cecilia. I thought of you constantly, but I didn't realize how much my silence would hurt you. I convinced myself you'd understand without needing an explanation. I was wrong."

She glanced at the crumpled cone in her hands, her voice trembling. "You didn't realize because you didn't think. It was thoughtless, Devin. And disrespectful. I expect better from the man I planned to marry."

The lash of her words left him momentarily speechless. "You're right," he said finally. "I should have written. I was so consumed with proving myself, I let you feel abandoned. I see that now."

Her expression softened slightly, though her eyes remained wary. "Why didn't you tell me about your plans? About how hard you were working? Did you think I wouldn't support you?"

"I didn't want to burden you," he admitted. "I didn't want you to worry. I thought if I worked harder and faster, I could make our future come sooner. I should have shared my struggles with you."

She studied him, her fingers smoothing the crumpled paper cone. "I don't know if I can trust you, Devin. It's not just about the letters. It's about knowing you'll stand by me no matter what."

"I will," he said fervently. "You have my word. Just give me the chance to prove it."

Before she could respond, the library door opened, and his mother swept in.

"Lady Cecilia," Lady Vincent exclaimed, her tone overly bright but laced with unmistakable strain. Her sharp gaze darted between them, widening ever so slightly as she took in the compromising sight of the two of them alone in the library. "There you are. I've been looking for you everywhere. How fortunate I found you before... well, before anyone else did." Her lips tightened briefly, then stretched into a thin smile. "I've decided it's time to put up the tree, and I simply must have your opinion on where to place it."

"Of course, Lady Vincent," Cecilia said, her tone polite but distant. She glanced at Devin, apology flickering in her eyes, before turning toward his mother.

She took Cecilia by the arm and led her from the room. At the doorway, she cast a sharp glance back at Devin.

If looks could wound, her glare would have felled him where he stood.

$$\maltese \quad 7 \quad \maltese$$

Devin

Not wanting anyone to know he'd been alone with Cecilia and draw the wrong conclusion, Devin decided to remain in the library for a while. It was easy enough to browse through the shelves and locate his father's new additions to the collection. He was surprised to find *The Raven and Other Poems* by that American, Edgar Allan Poe. He started reading it, and quickly found himself deeply engrossed. When he finally shook himself free of sad tale of "The Raven," he found that fifteen minutes had passed. It should be safe to return to the drawing room now. He found it difficult to shake off the feeling of loss that the poem had left him with.

When he stepped into the hallway, Horace nearly collided with him. He was fastidiously brushing at the sleeve of his dark jacket, not looking where he was going.

"Watch your step," Devin said.

"There you are. I could have used your help ten minutes ago. Mother had me put up the tree now instead of waiting until this evening. She decided it would be easier to decorate it in the daylight."

"What happened there?" Devin asked, gesturing toward a dark spot on Horace's sleeve.

"Pine sap. I need to change."

Devin grinned. "I'm sorry to have missed it. Well, perhaps not the pine sap."

"Pine sap is better than what you have in store. Mother's looking for you, and she's in a mood." Horace grinned as he headed for the staircase.

The hum of conversation and bursts of laughter drew him toward the drawing room, where the scent of cinnamon, cloves, and pine hung heavy in the air.

The room buzzed with activity. Guests crowded around tables scattered with paper, ribbons, and baubles, while children darted about with ornaments in hand. Large wooden boxes spilled their glittering contents across the floor—Mother's prized collection of Christmas decorations, gathered with near-obsessive enthusiasm ever since Queen Victoria had popularized the tradition.

Devin's gaze landed on Cecilia. She crouched beside one of the Marchcomb twins—the girl—helping her hang ornaments on the tree's lower branches. Her soft pink gown glowed in the candlelight, and when she turned to lift the little girl higher, her laughter rippled through the room, warming him like sunlight breaking through clouds.

The sight of her filled him with equal parts longing and frustration. His mother hovered nearby, her sharp gaze tracking Cecilia's every move. It wasn't the tree she cared about—it was control. Devin clenched his jaw. His mother's machinations were growing harder to ignore.

A flash of motion drew his attention to a young man seated with a sketchpad propped on his knee. Out of curiosity, Devin maneuvered closer, glancing over the artist's shoulder.

The sketches were remarkable—quick, fluid strokes that captured the room's lively chaos with stunning precision. Devin recognized several of the guests, their likenesses so vivid they seemed ready to step off the page.

"Those are excellent," Devin remarked.

The artist glanced up, startled, then smiled. "Thank you. I find people are most themselves in moments like this. It's the perfect opportunity to capture something real."

Devin gestured toward Cecilia. "The young woman by the tree —do you have a sketch of her?"

The artist flipped back a page, revealing a series of drawings. Cecilia's expressive face filled each frame, her warmth and grace practically glowing from the paper.

"Do you think you could draw a small portrait of her? Something about an inch high. One of myself as well."

"Certainly." The artist turned to a fresh page, pencil already moving. Devin nodded his thanks and left him to his work.

Across the room, that same little girl giggled and threw her arms around Cecilia's neck in an exuberant hug before darting away

Devin's chest tightened. She'd make a marvelous mother someday.

When Cecilia moved to collect another tree decorations, Lady Vincent followed, her every motion crisp and purposeful. Cecilia, ever quick-witted, mimed a dramatic tug on an invisible tether binding her wrist to Lady Vincent. She staggered forward in exaggerated obedience, her entire body seeming to strain under the invisible pull.

Devin grinned, then clamped a hand over his mouth. A single muffled burst of laughter escaped, which he hurriedly disguised as a cough.

His mother's sharp gaze zeroed in on him instantly. She strode over, her skirts swishing with determination.

Cecilia arched a brow at Lady Vincent's retreating back, then pretended her manacles had fallen away. She threw Devin a look that managed to convey both exasperation and amusement.

"Devin, there you are," his mother said said, her tone overly bright but underpinned with steel. "Mr. Glassford is waiting for a partner at whist. Your father is unavailable, so you'll take his place."

Devin glanced at Cecilia, who arched a curious eyebrow.

Devin forced a smile. "Of course, Mother. Lead the way."

A moment later, his mother introduced him to Mr. Glassford. "I hope you don't mind if I abandon you," she said. "I want to finish trimming the tree before dinner."

"Of course, Lady Vincent. Don't let me keep you," Mr. Glassford said as he turned to Devin. "Come. We've already claimed a table." He guided Devin toward a card table where Lady Judith Glassford and Miss Glassford were already seated. A moment later, Devin found himself sitting directly across from Miss Glassford. Fortunately, he also had an direct view of Cecilia.

Cecilia's gaze fixed on Miss Glassford's back for a moment, and then she scowled and turned her back on him.

Damn.

"Miss Glassford," Devin said, easing into the role of host with practiced politeness. "It's a pleasure to see you again. I trust you're enjoying your stay?"

She blushed faintly, her smile demure. "Absolutely. The visit has been lovely."

"Have you considered helping with the tree?" Devin asked, glancing toward the lively activity around the towering evergreen.

"Pine sap," Lady Judith interjected with an air of portent, brushing at her sleeve as if the mere thought sullied her clothing.

"And pine needles," Miss Glassford added, rubbing her hands together delicately as though imagining their sting. "It's dreadfully hard on one's gloves. I must admit, I don't understand why everyone insists on dragging live trees into their homes."

"Queen Victoria's influence," Devin mused. "Prince Albert brought the tradition from Germany, and the country followed suit."

"We aren't Germans," Miss Glassford said with a faint pout. "I can't see why we must adopt every custom they cherish."

Devin's mother, no longer hovering near Cecilia, turned her attention sharply toward the card table, her focus shifting entirely to Devin and his company. The game began with predictable monotony.

Mr. and Lady Judith Glassford played with effortless precision, their movements synchronized by years of practice. In stark contrast, Miss Glassford fumbled through the hands, her focus more on conversation than strategy.

"Do you know," she said, her voice lilting with affected charm, "I was disappointed to learn I won't be sitting near you at dinner tonight. I'd hoped to spend more time in your company."

Devin offered a polite nod, his mind drifting elsewhere. His gaze slipped past her shoulder, settling on Cecilia. She stood by the tree, helping a child hang a red cornucopia on the higher branches. The little boy threw his arms around Cecilia's neck in an exuberant hug before wriggling free and darting off to join his family.

"I've known Lady Cecilia since we were children," Devin said, almost without thinking, his words carrying a wistful undercurrent. "We've spent every Christmas together for years. I can't imagine the season without her."

Miss Glassford stiffened, her expression faltering. "Oh, my. I hadn't realized you were so... close."

Her voice trailed off, her words thin and uncertain. Devin watched the dawning comprehension sweep over her, the color draining from her cheeks. Her next card landed on the table askew, and she fumbled to correct it.

Lady Judith, ever vigilant, glanced between her daughter and Devin with a jaw set like steel. Though she said nothing, the tension in her expression spoke volumes.

Devin's mother, who had only moments ago been absorbed in tree trimming, now focused intently on the card table. Her eyes, sharp and calculating, flickered between the players as her expression soured from expectant to frustrated.

What had she hoped for? Devin had known from the start she was orchestrating his proximity to Miss Glassford, undoubtedly spinning tales about his desperate need for a wife. The right sort of wife.

The game dragged on, the mood at the table growing more stilted. Miss Glassford, her earlier coyness replaced by a strained silence, excused herself after their loss, her cheeks flushed with embarrassment. Lady Judith rose with her, murmuring some excuse as they departed together.

Devin's gaze lingered on their retreat before shifting to his mother. Her expression, once sharp with determination, now held the faintest flicker of irritation. Another plan disrupted. Another pawn slipping from her grasp.

He looked back to Cecilia. She crouched to help more children hang their ornaments, her soft laughter rising above the hum of the room. When she glanced his way, amusement flickered in her eyes, as though she understood all too well the tug-of-war playing out around them.

That single look, brimming with humor and understanding, sent a pang through him. She made enduring his mother's schemes almost bearable.

Devin exhaled slowly, forcing himself to refocus on the scattered cards before him. Confronting his mother outright wouldn't solve anything—not yet. This required strategy, careful unraveling.

Her schemes had grown too tangled to resolve in one confrontation. But one thing was certain: if he wanted a future with Cecilia, he'd need to untangle them before it was too late.

❦ 8 ❧

Cecilia

Miss Glassford moved toward the door with the unhurried ease of a woman who had never once doubted her own welcome. She radiated the kind of elegance Cecilia did not possess.

Watching Devin spend time with her gnawed at Cecilia, jealousy coiling in her chest. It was an ugly emotion, but undeniable. The fact that it had taken root told her one thing—things between her and Devin were far from resolved.

She had other things to resolve as well. Evangeline's words had been sitting at the back of her mind since yesterday—Babbage never suspected—patient and cold, waiting for her to find the right moment. She had been watching for her opportunity. She had not yet found it. But the Glassfords' room sat empty at the end of the upper corridor, and Mr. Glassford had been downstairs all morning.

Soon.

His explanation for his silence rang true, but it also revealed a troubling flaw: a blind spot to her perspective, to how his actions —or lack thereof—might affect her. She had accepted his reasoning. She had not stopped wondering whether it would happen again.

The sound of Lady Vincent's voice pulled Cecilia from her thoughts.

"Lady Judith, would you like to join us?" Lady Vincent asked, her tone almost warm. "We're nearly finished trimming the tree."

"No, thank you. I'm sure you're managing beautifully. I couldn't possibly improve upon such perfection." Lady Judith folded her hands with a polite smile.

"How are you finding your new home? Settling in well?"

"We're making improvements. Mr. Glassford is adding a new wing for indoor washrooms."

"How splendid! Your home will be quite the marvel."

"Indeed. But I'm far more interested in updating the stables. You know how I love to ride. I'm convincing Mr. Glassford to replace the entire building. The current one is wholly inadequate."

Cecilia placed an ornament as high as she could reach, glancing uneasily at the young man perched on a ladder above her. The tree wobbled slightly as he shifted to hang an ornament, and her heart jumped. She couldn't bear to watch.

A sudden commotion drew her attention. A little boy came barreling toward the tree, panic written across his small face.

"No! They're all gone! I didn't get to put one on the tree!" he wailed.

Lady Vincent's head snapped toward the boy, her expression icy. "What is the meaning of this disruption?" Her voice, calm and clipped, commanded the room's attention.

The child clung to her skirts, leaving faint smudges on the pristine silk. "I want to trim the tree too!" he cried, his small body trembling with distress.

Lady Vincent's lips thinned. She reached down, prying his fingers from the fabric with a sharp but measured grip. "Young man, a gentleman does not tug at a lady's gown." Her gaze remained fixed on him, cool and unyielding. "Had you arrived earlier, you might have had the opportunity to participate. As it is, you'll simply have to wait for another occasion."

Her attention shifted to the smudges on her skirt, and she let out a soft gasp. "What is this? Chocolate?"

Lady Judith stepped forward briskly. "What a bother. Rest assured, my lady's maid can clean it. Tomkins is a miracle worker when it comes to such things. I'll send her to you at once."

Lady Vincent's tone softened, but her grip on the boy's wrist remained firm. "Are you certain? My maid is quite useless when it comes to delicate fabrics."

"Absolutely. We'll see to it immediately."

Lady Vincent dropped the boy's wrist as if discarding a piece of rubbish and followed Lady Judith out of the room.

The boy stood frozen, his small frame shaking. "I didn't mean it," he whispered, tears streaking his cheeks.

Cecilia crouched to his level, her heart aching. "I know you didn't, sweeting. It's only a bit of chocolate. Everything will be fine, you'll see."

"But Lady Vincent's angry! What if she tells Papa? I'll get a thrashing." His voice wavered. "Papa said not to embarrass him."

Cecilia's heart tightened. She cupped the boy's face, brushing away his tears. "What's your name?"

"Douglas Marchcomb."

"I'm Lady Cecilia Paring. And I promise, everything will be fine."

She handed him the last red cornucopia. "Here, Douglas. Would you like to hang this on the tree?"

His wide, tear-filled eyes brightened. "May I?"

"You certainly may. Where do you think it should go?"

He examined the tree carefully and then pointed to a bare branch just above her head. She lifted him, steadying him as he carefully hung the ornament. When the task was done, he beamed, his earlier tears forgotten.

Douglas scampered off to rejoin his mother, but she didn't appear to notice his arrival. He reached for her hand, only for her to yank it away with a sharp hiss. The child's face crumpled, and he fled the room.

Cecilia's chest tightened. She turned back to the tree.

The drawing room hummed around her—Lady Vincent's sharp voice somewhere behind her, the children's laughter, the smell of cinnamon and hot wax.

The Glassfords' room—hers and Evangeline's until this visit—was sitting empty at the end of the upper corridor, and Mr. Glassford was down here with everyone else. Perhaps she should take a leaf from her sister's book and do a bit of investigating herself. Surely a busy man like Mr. Glassford would not travel without correspondence.

Not now—there were too many people, too much movement, someone would notice her absence. But soon. Before dinner. She needed to find a moment when the corridor would be quiet.

She turned back toward the tree and waited for her opportunity.

Her thoughts drifted to Devin, to the way his presence still made her heart ache. She couldn't be happy without him, but she also couldn't be with a man who might wound her so deeply again.

Cecilia inhaled deeply, steadying herself. She had to speak with Devin. They needed an agreement, a promise that he would treat her as his equal, his partner. Only then could she give him her heart without reservation.

She turned to examine the tree. It glimmered with red ribbons, silver ornaments, and pure white candles. Tonight, it would shine in its full glory, a moment of perfect beauty.

Resolving to return to her room, Cecilia stepped into the hallway. She'd barely taken a step when a firm hand grasped hers, pulling her into the nearby morning room.

Devin.

Her heart pounded as she faced him.

"I could barely keep my eyes off you," Devin said, his voice raw. "This is why I didn't write. Picturing you while I was so far away nearly broke me."

His words hit her like a tidal wave, stealing her breath.

Devin groaned, wrapping her in his arms and burying his face in her hair. His warmth chased away the chill of the empty room.

He kissed her neck, her cheek, and finally her lips.

Cecilia trembled, her resolve slipping. She wrapped her arms around him, falling into the kiss, into him.

This afternoon, she'd believed a moment like this would never happen again. When she'd broken things off, she'd been convinced he'd never again hold her in his arms. Never kiss her. Never whisper her name.

"Cecilia," he murmured, his voice filled with longing.

Tears welled in her eyes. Did he truly mean to change? Could she trust him with her heart again?

A delicate cough interrupted them, and they sprang apart, breathless and startled.

❦   9   ❦

DEVIN

The abrupt change left Devin reeling. His suddenly empty arms ached to pull Cecilia back, but the appearance of a new threat forced him to pivot. He stepped forward instinctively, blocking Cecilia from view.

In the open doorway stood Lady Evangeline and Lady Elizabeth—with one hand covering her eyes. Relief coursed through him, though it was short-lived. Lady Elizabeth's reputation as a collector of gossip preceded her, and the mischievous glint in her green eyes suggested she had already begun filing away this scene for later use.

Devin stared at the young woman, uncertain whether to address her as a girl or a lady. Her riotous black curls tumbled down her back, and the hand she clamped dramatically over her eyes only made her seem younger—like a child playing at hide-and-seek. He half-expected her to start counting aloud.

"Oh, my, Evangeline," Lady Elizabeth declared, her voice mockingly exaggerated, "I've been struck by a sudden and tragic bout of blindness. I can't see a thing."

Lady Evangeline rolled her eyes and tugged Elizabeth's hand

away from her face. "It's safe now." She threw Devin a pointed glance. "And honestly, it's about time. You nearly broke my sister's heart with your thoughtlessness. You really should have written to her."

Relief made his knees weak. At least Cecilia's sister wasn't entirely against him.

Cecilia stepped out from behind him, her voice cool. "Were you looking for me?"

Lady Evangeline dismissed the question with a wave. "We were sneaking around, spying. You'd be shocked at the goings-on in a country house."

Elizabeth's eyes sparkled with glee. "We just caught Mr. Glassford shamelessly flirting with one of your mother's chambermaids. He had her pinned against the wall."

Evangeline's tone was light, almost careless. "We thought you should know. A man who behaves that way below stairs will bear watching." She glanced at Cecilia as she said it.

Cecilia met her sister's eyes briefly, then turned to Devin. "This is troubling behavior from a guest," she said, her voice perfectly pleasant. "One hopes it isn't indicative of his character more broadly."

Devin's stomach tightened. If his mother learned of this, she wouldn't consider confronting Mr. Glassford... it was the maid who would lose her position without a reference. "I'll handle it."

He glanced between the sisters. Something had passed between them—too quick and too practiced to be accidental—but he didn't ask.

Lady Elizabeth lifted her chin, skepticism clear in her expression. "How?"

"I'll make sure she stays below stairs for the rest of the week."

"That might not work." Elizabeth tilted her head, the arch of her eyebrow making her seem far older than her years. "She was near the kitchen when it happened. We'd gone to pilfer more gingerbread and saw them there."

"In that case, I'll warn Cook and Mrs. Rumsey," Devin said. The housekeeper, a formidable woman, would ensure Mr. Glassford didn't wander below stairs again. "If that doesn't work, I'll arrange for the maid to visit her family until his departure."

Elizabeth regarded him for a long moment, her gaze unexpectedly sharp. "You do that." She glanced at Cecilia, her playful demeanor shifting into something more serious. "You might also spend less time worrying about a maid's reputation and more about someone far dearer to you."

She turned and swept from the room, pulling Lady Evangeline along with her.

Devin frowned after her, disconcerted by the layers of meaning in her parting words. How had Elizabeth gained such a hard edge? Was it a result of her relentless spying, or had life already taught her lessons he wished she'd been spared?

A soft hand pressed against his chest, breaking his thoughts. Cecilia.

But instead of a caress, she pushed him aside and moved into the doorway, peering down the hall before spinning to face him.

"You can't just pull me into your arms and kiss me like that," she said, her voice low but firm. "I'm not yours. Not anymore."

Devin blinked, taken aback. "I thought we'd mended things."

Her sharp gaze made him feel like a schoolboy caught misbehaving. "You apologized," she said. "That's a start. But forgiveness doesn't mean I've forgotten how you hurt me. You took me for granted, Devin. If you truly want me as your wife, you'll need to win me back. Promise me you'll change, and then prove it."

Her words struck like a hammer, shattering any lingering illusions that their problems could be easily swept aside. Her resolve was unyielding, her pain visible in the way her lips pressed together to keep her composure.

He rocked back on his heels, scrambling for the right response. Everything hinged on this moment.

"You're right," he said, his voice steady despite the turmoil inside him. "What I did was callous and disrespectful. I see that now, and I promise I'll never hurt you like that again. I'll do whatever it takes to make it up to you. Let's begin again."

Cecilia stilled, her expression softening as the tension in her shoulders eased. After a moment, she nodded. "That's a good beginning."

She turned toward the hallway, then glanced over her shoulder. "Walk with me."

❧ 10 ❧

Devin

Devin matched Cecilia's measured pace as they made their way down the hallway toward the foyer. Each unhurried step felt like a stolen moment, and he wanted to stretch their time together as long as possible.

As the last rays of sunlight faded, moonlight poured through the window at the end of the corridor, casting everything in a silvery glow.

A footman entered, carrying a lighted taper. He paused at a niche, using it to ignite a nearby lamp, then moved on to the next.

Cecilia hesitated, her gaze following the man as he worked, but her distant expression told Devin she wasn't really seeing him. Her distraction gave him a chance to study her.

In the dim light, her gown appeared ivory, but as the footman lit each lamp, the warm glow restored the world's color: her soft pink dress, the rich chestnut of her hair, the golden undertones of her skin.

"For some reason," he said, breaking the silence, "seeing you in this light reminds me of the Christmas when you and your friends performed a pantomime in Grecian robes."

She blinked, surprised by the memory. "That was only three years ago."

"Three years? It feels longer. As I recall, Lady Elizabeth's friend Catherine wasn't pleased with the goddess you chose to portray."

Cecilia's lips curved into a faint smile. "That's because Catherine was being pedantic. My goddess wasn't Grecian but Roman, and she disapproved. I wanted to be Iustitia, the goddess of justice. You know how stubborn I can be. Justice is important to me. It's a virtue that's too often overlooked."

"You know I agree. Justice is the cornerstone of modern government."

Her expression softened. "It's a shame we haven't learned to apply it fairly. I've seen too much of its absence firsthand. I mentioned in my letters that I've been visiting orphanages in the county. Our so-called justice system abandons those children, leaving them prey to anyone bigger or stronger."

The footman disappeared into the main salon, and Cecilia resumed walking.

"I admire you for what you're doing," Devin said, guilt twisting in his chest. Her letters about the orphanages had gone unanswered. Her words had been full of purpose, and he'd failed to acknowledge them.

He hesitated, then added, "I hadn't realized your mother still visits the orphanages. It must be taxing for her, given her health."

"She isn't always well enough to join me," Cecilia admitted.

Devin frowned. "Visiting the orphanages is admirable, Cecilia, but have you considered the toll it takes on both you and your mother? It's not just about safety—it's about preserving your strength. Those children depend on you. If you exhaust yourself, how will you continue to help them?"

She paused mid-step and turned to face him. Her eyes narrowed, though not with anger—more with caution. "And what would you have me do? Turn my back on them? Tell them I'm too fragile to face their struggles?"

He shook his head. "No, that's not what I mean at all. You're stronger than anyone I know. But even the strongest among us need rest and care. If you overtax yourself, what good will that do? You'll be less able to help them, and you'll harm yourself in the process."

For a moment, her guard slipped, and he caught a flicker of vulnerability. "I've never thought of it like that," she admitted quietly. "I don't want to stop helping them, but I do feel... weary at times. Like the weight of it all is pressing down on me."

"That's what I'm saying," Devin said gently. "You don't have to bear it all alone. Share the burden with others who can help. Let me help."

She studied him for a long moment, her gaze searching his face. "You would do that?"

"In an instant," he said firmly. "I want to support you, Cecilia. In every way I can. But you must promise me you'll also look after yourself."

She glanced away, her expression tightening. "I will." After a beat, she added, "Since my father's situation has changed, it's harder to help the orphans as much as I'd like. I can still place older girls as kitchen help or shop assistants, but my resources are limited."

"I can help with that," Devin said. "I have connections with some of the counting houses nearby. They're always looking for clever boys with a knack for numbers."

Her face lit up, the transformation breathtaking. "Oh, Devin, that would be wonderful. Would you truly do that?"

"Of course," he said simply. Anything to keep that radiant smile on her face.

Encouraged, she placed a hand on his arm. "Perhaps you can help with another problem."

She explained the situation with Douglas Marchcomb,

recounting the boy's fear of punishment for soiling his mother's gown. As she spoke, Devin began to understand the depth of her concern.

"You want me to intercede?"

Her shoulders tensed. "You know I can't. If I approach your mother, it'll only make things worse."

"Undoubtedly." He grinned, trying to lighten her mood. "Don't worry. I'll make sure Douglas gets his Christmas."

It was the first genuine smile he'd seen from her all day.

They reached the foyer, and Cecilia tucked her hand into the crook of his arm. She was quiet for a moment — a different kind of quiet than before, considered rather than distant. He had the sense she was choosing her words.

She glanced up at him. "Devin, there's something I need to—"

"Devin. Just the person I was looking for."

His mother's voice cut across the foyer. Lady Vincent descended the staircase, her gaze locking onto Cecilia's hand against his jacket. Her sharp smile didn't reach her eyes.

Cecilia withdrew her hand, her warmth gone in an instant.

"It would be my pleasure," he lied.

He fell into step behind his mother, his jaw tight. Cecilia had been about to tell him something—he'd heard it in her voice, felt it in the particular quality of her silence before she spoke. And now it was gone, the moment closed off as neatly as a door being shut in his face.

His mother was saying something about his father and the library. He made the appropriate sounds of agreement.

It was not the first time today she had done this. He was finally realizing it wouldn't be the last.

❧ I I ☙

Cecilia

Cecilia climbed the stairs slowly, glancing back over her shoulder as Lady Vincent leaned in close to Devin, whispering something in his ear. Whatever she said was inaudible, but the way she steered him down the hallway spoke volumes. Cecilia couldn't help but wonder if the conversation had anything to do with young Douglas.

She had been about to confide in him about Glassford. His mother had seen to it that she couldn't. Again.

As Devin disappeared from view, doubts about him crept back into her thoughts. Could he truly change? People rarely altered their core nature unless they saw the need for it themselves. Her mother's cautionary words from years ago echoed in her mind: *"Cecilia, don't marry a man expecting to change him. The flaws he has at the start will only grow with time. Decide if you can live with them, because they'll become a permanent fixture in your life."*

At the time, her mother's advice had felt like a thinly veiled critique of her father's gullible optimism. He'd been a man who believed in luck and charm, traits that made him an easy target for schemers. Yet her mother hadn't chosen bitterness. She'd accepted his nature, finding ways to navigate around his weaknesses while appreciating his strengths.

Now Cecilia saw the wisdom in those words as something broader. Her mother hadn't just chosen a husband—she'd chosen the life she would lead under his care. As a woman in this world, there was little else she could control. Love might have been part of the equation, but it had to be balanced with respect and trust.

Could she respect Devin after he had so thoughtlessly ignored her feelings? Could she trust him not to retreat into himself, valuing his own ambitions over their partnership?

Over time, Father had grown more cautious, each financial setback serving as a hard-earned lesson. Treachery, once invisible to his hopeful eyes, now seemed to lurk around every corner. Though he still sought a way out of his current difficulties, he no longer blindly trusted those peddling schemes. Instead, he scrutinized them as he should have all along. How successful had their past ventures been? What did previous investors say about them? Were there suspicious gaps in their history that might conceal substantial losses?

He'd learned to steer clear of the most obvious schemes. Instead, he'd staked everything on a single daring venture—a fast ship laden with sugar. If all had gone as planned, the gamble would have paid off handsomely. But it hadn't. The ship had taken on water, and the entire shipment had been ruined.

That failure had driven him to search for a new investment, "something bold," he'd said. Something he could control, free from the whims and failures of others.

She stopped walking.

She had been turning Devin over in her mind all day—his silences, his apologies, his promises—and it had gotten her precisely nowhere. She could keep turning him over until dinner and still not know whether to believe him. But this—the Glassfords, the Mediterranean Mercantile, Evangeline's certainty—this was something she could actually *do* something about. The corridor was quiet. The guests were all below. This was the moment.

She moved past her own room and walked to the end of the corridor.

She knocked on the Glassfords' door. When no answer came, she tried the handle.

It opened.

She stood in the doorway for a moment, listening to the sounds of the guests below her.

Then she stepped inside and pulled the door nearly shut behind her, leaving it an inch ajar so she would hear footsteps on the stairs.

The room was as she remembered. The writing desk beneath the window. A traveling case on the table. The small chair angled toward the fire, which had burned low in the family's absence.

She dropped her gloves near the door. If anyone discovered her here, she was not searching his belongings. She was merely searching for her gloves which she dropped when she'd wandered in earlier.

She crossed to the writing desk and found a letter lying in the center, a pot of ink and pen next to it.

Beside it lay a second sheet of paper, both held flat by the weight of a small brass paperweight. The top letter was written in a fine continental hand, the date at the upper right catching her eye immediately.

Paris, December 18, 1850.

Six days ago.

Her breath caught when her eyes skimmed and she saw the words Mediterranean Mercantile. It couldn't be this easy, could it?

She read.

My dear Glassford,

Your position advances most satisfactorily. The Babbage family has not recovered from the dissolution of the Mediterranean Mercantile—nor, I think, will they. The father grows more desperate with each passing season, and the rumors you have seeded regarding the family's misfortunes have taken root admirably. Society, as ever, requires little encouragement to believe in a curse where there is merely ruin.

The Vincent match remains your surest path. The countess is receptive —more so than she might otherwise have been, had the Babbage girl remained a credible prospect. Push the advantage while it holds.

The Babbage girl. A flash of anger—brief, bright—and then she read on.

As for the matter of the elder son—I would not act hastily. You must gather information first. But it is worth noting that the younger Montlake, as a second son, inherits nothing of consequence. Were that circumstance to change, your daughter's position would be of an entirely different order. I leave the consideration to you.

Your servant in this, H. Voclain

She set the letter down.

For a moment she couldn't move. The deliberateness of it. Her father hadn't met with random misfortune. Their financial circumstances had nothing to do with his weakness but were attributable to a man sitting in a Paris office writing instructions as calmly as if he were ordering furniture. Her chest tightened with a fury she hadn't known she was capable of. Her family had spent a year economizing, worrying, quietly diminishing, and somewhere across the Channel H. Voclain had been satisfied with how things were progressing.

She picked up the second sheet. It was shorter, unfinished, the ink fresh. A different hand than Voclain's, likely Glassford's reply... or a draft of it.

Voclain —

Progress is satisfactory. Lady V. has proved most cooperative, and the girl's prospects among the local families have been thoroughly

It ended there, mid-sentence. And in the margin, cramped and slightly apart from each other as though written at different moments:

H.—hunter? riding habits?

The fury went out of her like a candle in a draught, leaving her breathless.

Horace. Cheerful, kind Horace who had teased her about her rosy cheeks and wild ways when she'd been a child. Who'd hauled a Christmas tree through the front door with pine sap on his sleeve. Glassford was plotting to kill him. Not in so many words—not yet—but that was the shape of it, that was what those two careful questions were reaching toward, and the coldness that moved through her now had nothing to do with the dying fire.

She stood very still, and underneath the stillness something that was not quite fear and not quite calm held her in place while the laughter of children drifted up from the floor below.

She picked up both sheets and folded them carefully—Voclain's letter first, then the unfinished draft. She tucked them inside her bodice, against her stays where they would not shift.

She looked at the desk. It appeared exactly as she had found it, the brass paperweight sitting where it had been, the surface otherwise undisturbed. Glassford would know the letters were gone. There was nothing to be done about that.

She retrieved her gloves from the floor and clutched them tightly.

Then she stood for a moment in the middle of the room, in the fading afternoon light, and thought about what she was going to do.

She could go to her father. She knew immediately and with complete certainty that she would not. Her mother was too frail; her father would either collapse under the weight of this or rage his way into a public scene that would destroy them more thoroughly than Glassford had managed. Either way, her mother would suffer. That door was closed.

She could go to Devin. The thought arrived with a warmth she didn't entirely trust—not because she doubted him, but because she doubted herself. She wanted to go to Devin. She wanted to hand this to him and let his barrister's mind work through it and determine what to do. That wanting was precisely why she wouldn't. Not yet. She would not arrive at Devin's side as a woman who needed rescuing. Not when she hadn't yet tried to rescue herself.

She could go to Glassford.

She turned the idea over. He would be larger than her, older than her, more practiced in the particular art of looking at a person and seeing only what they were worth to him. He had defrauded her father without compunction. He was considering something worse.

And she had his letters.

She straightened her shoulders, tucked her gloves into her pocket, and opened the door.

She would need Evangeline.

❧

THE DRAWING ROOM WAS BRIGHT WITH CANDLELIGHT AND loud with the particular hum of guests who had been confined indoors all day and were growing restless before dinner. Cecilia stood near the doorway with Evangeline, watching.

"There," Evangeline murmured. "He's moving."

Mr. Glassford had disengaged himself from a conversation near the fireplace and was making his way toward the door—heading, Cecilia judged, for the corridor. Perhaps the library. This was the perfect opportunity.

"Go," Cecilia said.

Evangeline didn't need telling twice. She slipped into the drawing room with practiced ease. She'd been moving through spaces like these since she was old enough to walk. Within moments she stood at Lady Judith's elbow, her expression one of bright and entirely feigned social interest.

Cecilia didn't wait to watch. She moved after Glassford.

She caught him in the corridor, just outside the morning room door.

"Mr. Glassford." Her voice was pleasant. "I wonder if I might speak with you."

He turned. When he recognized her, his expression shifted—something carefully composed settling over him. He was quick. A practiced liar.

"Lady Cecilia." A measured smile. "Of course."

She opened the morning room door and waited. After a moment's hesitation—just long enough to tell her he was granting her an audience at his own discretion—he went in. She followed and left the door open—for propriety's sake. Voices from the drawing room drifted through, faint but present. Witnesses, of a kind. Neither of them would be able to make a scene.

He stood near the window, the fading light behind him. A tactical position—it put his face in shadow and required her to look toward the light. She noted it without reacting and moved to stand beside the fireplace instead, where the light was even.

"I'll be brief," she said. "I think that's best for both of us."

She reached into her bodice and withdrew both sheets. She held them out just long enough for him to see what they were—Voclain's letter and the beginnings of his freshly drafted reply—and watched his face.

He went very still.

She tucked them away. Swiftly. Smoothly. Putting them beyond his reach in her bodice. Safe, since she was certain he wouldn't make the kind of scene neither of them could afford.

"You've been busy," she said. "I'll give you that."

"Those are my private—"

"Yes," she agreed. "They are. Which makes it all the more interesting that I found them on your writing desk." She kept her voice mild. "I don't intend to discuss the details of what's in them. We both know exactly what they say."

He looked at her for a long moment. She could see him calculating: her age, her rank, how much power she had—or had access to, whether she was bluffing. She met his gaze and waited.

"You're very composed," he said at last, "for a girl of seventeen."

If that was meant to rattle her, he'd need to try harder. "I've had practice." She paused. "Mr. Montlake has also seen the letters."

Something moved in his expression—not quite fear, not quite anger. Something more complicated than either. She couldn't let herself be distracted wondering what it meant.

"He's a barrister," she continued. "A good one, as I'm certain you know. He found the contents quite instructive regarding the Mediterranean Mercantile Company. He says he knows where to look, and I don't doubt he'll find something." She let that settle. "I thought you should know."

He reassessed her now, and she had the impression it was because she'd surprised him. "What is it you want?" His voice had changed—flatter, more careful.

"Very little, actually." She folded her hands. "The rumors about my family must stop. I believe you know the ones I mean— the talk of curses, of bad luck, of my father's failures. They stop. Today. You do what you can to repair the damage they've cause."

He said nothing.

"And your family departs after Christmas as planned, without any further interest in the affairs of the Babbages, the Vincent household, or its guests." She paused. "That's all."

He blinked, then stared at her for a long moment—that assessing look, the one that wanted to find a weakness. She kept her expression pleasant and her shoulders still.

"And?"

"That's all," she repeated.

"What if I decline to allow a child to correct my behavior?"

"Then Mr. Montlake pursues his inquiry." She said it simply, without heat. "He's thorough. He *will* find things." She tilted her head slightly. "I imagine the dissolution of the Mediterranean Mercantile left certain records. Ledgers. Legal documents. Correspondence. The sort of thing that's difficult to find and eliminate."

The silence stretched. From the drawing room came a burst of youthful laughter—Evangeline, she thought, maintaining the distraction.

Glassford looked away first.

It was not a dramatic capitulation. There was no outburst, no threat, no plea. He simply looked toward the window for a moment, his jaw tight, and then looked back at her with the expression of a man who had made the calculations and found the answer disagreeable.

"The rumors," he said carefully, "have perhaps been allowed to spread further than was wise."

"Yes," she agreed. "They have."

Another silence. "I see no reason our visit should extend beyond Boxing Day."

"Nor do I."

He inclined his head—a stiff, minimal thing. She returned it. They understood each other.

He spoke before she could move. "My daughter's regard for Mr. Montlake is her own affair." His voice was even, almost polite. "I trust you understand that is not part of our agreement."

Cecilia held his gaze for a moment. "I understand perfectly."

She moved to the door, then paused with her hand on the frame. "One more thing." She kept her back to him, afraid she'd lose her courage if she looked him in the eye. "Mr. Montlake is also aware of the notes you wrote in the reply you drafted regarding Horace." She kept her voice entirely even. "He takes a particular interest in his brother's welfare. As do I." A beat. "I thought that was also worth mentioning."

She left before he could respond.

THE CORRIDOR WAS EMPTY. SHE WALKED TO THE FAR END OF IT, turned the corner, and stood with her back against the wall.

Her hands were shaking.

She pressed them flat against her skirts and breathed—one slow breath, then another—until the shaking stopped. It took longer than she would have liked.

She had been terrified the entire time. He had not seen it. At least—she was fairly certain he had not seen it.

She stood straight, lifted her chin, smoothed her skirts, and went to find her sister.

Evangeline spotted her through the drawing room door and immediately extricated herself from Lady Judith. She took one look at Cecilia's face and merely asked, "Well?"

"It's handled."

Evangeline studied her for a moment with that look—the one that made Cecilia feel like the younger of the two. Then she nodded, once, and offered her arm.

They went upstairs to prepare for dinner.

12

DEVIN

Devin leaned against the marble mantel of the fireplace, the heat of the crackling flames doing little to soothe the tension coiled in his chest. The drawing room buzzed with subdued activity. Guests chatted in small groups beneath the towering Christmas tree, its branches adorned with ribbons and baubles, yet the festive air did nothing to ease the knot of unease tightening in his gut.

He forced his attention to the room, scanning for Cecilia. When he spotted her entering with her father, her gaze swept over the crowd before settling on him. Something in his chest unclenched, if only slightly. She looked poised, the golden light from the chandelier casting a warm glow over her hair and softening the edges of her resolute expression.

Horace approached, cutting across his line of sight with a grim look. "Were you here earlier, when Mother was trimming the tree?"

Devin raised a brow. "What's she angry about now?" He didn't need to ask if she was angry—Lady Vincent's wrath was as predictable as the turning of the seasons.

"She's claiming Lady Marchcomb's nanny is to blame for the chocolate handprints," Horace said, his voice low but tight. "She's insisting the woman didn't 'control' the boy properly."

Devin's jaw tightened, the familiar flare of frustration rising. "So she wants to ruin a woman's livelihood over a child being, well, a child? That's a new low."

Horace nodded, his mouth thinning. "She's already making noise about Lady Marchcomb needing to dismiss her."

Devin exhaled sharply, a mix of anger and resignation swirling in his chest. "I'll speak to her. This ends tonight."

Horace gave him a skeptical look. "You know how she is. She'll dig her heels in just to make a point."

Devin glanced toward Cecilia, who had moved closer to the table of ornaments, idly tracing a fingertip over the gilded edge of a cornucopia. Her expression held a shadow of worry, though her shoulders remained squared.

"I don't care," Devin said firmly, his gaze snapping back to his brother. "This isn't just about the nanny—it's about showing her she can't run roughshod over everyone. If I don't push back, she'll think she can keep doing it."

Horace sighed. "Well, good luck. You'll need it."

Devin didn't respond. Instead, he straightened as Lady Vincent swept into the room, her emerald-green velvet gown swirling with authority. Her face was set, her lips pressed into a thin line, and her eyes glinted with the sharpness of a blade. Trouble, as always, arrived in her wake.

"Devin," she called, her voice slicing through the hum of conversation. "A word."

He glanced at Cecilia, catching the flicker of tension in her expression before she quickly masked it. She looked as though she wanted to speak, to stop him, but he shook his head almost imperceptibly. Stay out of this, his eyes said.

He moved to intercept his mother before she reached Cecilia, summoning every ounce of composure he had. "Mother, you look particularly elegant tonight," he said, his tone smooth, though his jaw was tight. "Father will be proud to have you preside over his table this evening."

Lady Vincent's sharp gaze lingered on him, as if trying to parse out the sincerity behind his words. After a moment, her shoulders relaxed slightly. "Thank you, Devin. It's nice to know someone in this family appreciates my efforts."

Devin offered a faint smile, but his reprieve was short-lived. Lady Vincent's eyes flicked past him to where Cecilia stood with Lord Babbage, her posture perfectly composed.

"Lady Cecilia," Lady Vincent called. "Join us."

Cecilia approached with a calm grace that made Devin's chest ache with pride and worry in equal measure. She stopped just short of Lady Vincent, her chin lifted.

"You were there earlier, were you not?" Lady Vincent said, her voice smooth but edged with accusation. "When that boy soiled my gown?"

"I was," Cecilia replied evenly. "Standing right next to you."

Lady Vincent narrowed her eyes. "Then you know he acted out of malice. The gleam in his eye made it perfectly clear."

Cecilia tilted her head, her calm composure unshaken. "I didn't see malice, Lady Vincent. I only saw a distressed child who wanted to trim the tree."

Devin saw his mother's nostrils flare, her sharp gaze flicking to Cecilia as though searching for a crack in her armor. "Distressed? His behavior was intentional, I assure you. That nanny of his failed completely in her duties."

Cecilia's expression softened, but her tone remained firm. "Even the best-behaved children can act out when they feel excluded. The boy seemed heartbroken when he thought he'd missed his chance to participate."

Lady Vincent's lips pressed into a thin line. "Heartbroken or not, his actions caused harm. The nanny should have prevented it."

Devin stepped in, his voice calm but resolute. "Mother, I'll address it. There's no need to escalate this further."

Lady Vincent shot him a sharp look but said nothing, clearly debating whether to push the matter. As if sensing the tension, Cecilia inclined her head and spoke with quiet grace. "If you'll excuse me, I think I'm needed elsewhere." Without waiting for a reply, she inclined her head and turned away, her steps measured as she crossed the room to rejoin her father.

Devin followed her departure with his eyes, his jaw tightening. He didn't miss the flicker of irritation that crossed his mother's face as Cecilia left, but the moment passed quickly. Lady Vincent turned her focus back to him, her expression sharp.

"Perhaps if you hadn't been so forthright with Miss Glassford, you'd have more credibility with me," she said, her tone cold.

Devin blinked, caught off guard. "Miss Glassford?"

"Don't play coy," she snapped. "Emphasizing your lifelong acquaintance with Lady Cecilia during whist was entirely unnecessary. You embarrassed Miss Glassford and gave her family reason to question our hospitality."

Devin folded his arms, his expression hardening. "If Miss Glassford felt slighted, that's because you manipulated the situation. Don't blame me for the consequences."

Lady Vincent's lips thinned into a razor-sharp line. "I'll need you to escort Miss Glassford to dinner tonight. Her mother requested it specifically, and after the assistance she's provided, I can't refuse."

Devin's gaze flicked toward Cecilia, now deep in conversation with her father. His jaw tightened. "I'm escorting Lady Cecilia. I'm not a pawn for you to move around as you please."

Lady Vincent's eyes narrowed to slits. "You've always been obstinate, Devin. Perhaps it's time you learned the cost of your defiance."

Horace stepped in quickly, his voice placating. "Mother, this isn't the time—"

She cut him off, her voice icy. "Escort Miss Glassford, Devin. If you refuse, then your father and I are done with you."

Her words landed like a blow, the cold finality in her tone leaving no room for misinterpretation. Without waiting for a response, she turned and swept out of the room, her skirts rustling like a storm in her wake.

Devin stared after her, his jaw clenched. Horace let out a low whistle, his face pale. "What the hell just happened?"

Devin exhaled slowly, his gaze sliding to Cecilia. She was laughing softly at something her father had said, her face glowing with warmth and light.

"She thinks she's won," he said quietly, his voice steely. "But this isn't over."

13

C ECILIA

As Cecilia paused near the Christmas tree, her fingers brushed the edge of a delicate silver ornament. The tension in the room was palpable, though most of the guests remained oblivious. Across the room, Lady Vincent swept away from Devin and Horace, her sharp gestures betraying her temper. A moment later, Devin was crossing toward her.

"Cecilia," he said quietly, stopping just short of her. His voice was low, almost apologetic. "I need to tell you something before dinner."

Her stomach tightened at his tone. "What is it?"

He exhaled sharply, his gaze flicking toward the far end of the room, where Lady Vincent stood, her sharp gaze sweeping over the guests. "Mother has insisted I escort Miss Glassford tonight."

Cecilia's chest constricted, but she forced her voice to remain even. "I see. And you're complying, of course."

His jaw tightened, and a flicker of frustration passed over his face. "I don't have a choice. If I refuse her now, she'll make things worse—for the Marchcomb situation, for you, for everyone."

Cecilia studied him, searching for a trace of the man who had once seemed so unshakable. "You're saying this is about pragmatism."

"It's about strategy," he corrected, his tone firm. "I need you to trust me on this."

She wanted to believe him, but the ache in her chest wouldn't relent. "Very well," she said finally, her voice quieter than she intended. "If you think it's best."

"Cecilia—" He stepped closer, his hand almost reaching for hers before he stopped himself. "This isn't what I want. You know that."

She nodded stiffly, unwilling to let him see how much his words affected her. "I understand."

Devin's lips pressed into a thin line, as though he wanted to say more but couldn't. Finally, he inclined his head and stepped back. "We'll talk later."

Cecilia watched him go, her heart sinking further with every step he took. She turned away, blinking back the sting of unshed tears, and spotted her father standing near the hearth. His tall figure was a familiar anchor, and she moved toward him, hoping his steady presence would ease her disappointment.

"Thank you again for warning me about that nonsense rumor regarding a curse," her father said as soon as he spotted her. "Lord Marchcomb brought it up earlier, but I set him straight. Still, I can't keep fighting this battle one person at a time. Rumors travel faster than the truth, especially when the truth is far less interesting."

"What will you do?" Cecilia asked, sliding a comforting arm through his.

"I have a plan to shift the conversation entirely," he said, touching the side of his nose with a conspiratorial grin. "Just wait and see."

Her lips twitched, though she wasn't reassured. She'd seen her father's bravado before, and it often led to chaos rather than solutions. "I hope your plan works."

She meant it more than he knew. Glassford had agreed to stop seeding the rumors—but rumors did not stop the moment their source fell silent. They travelled on their own momentum, passed along by people who had no idea where they had come from. Her father was still fighting the damage of something that was already done. That was not Glassford's failure to keep his word. Gossip had a life of its own.

She watched her father touch the side of his nose with that familiar conspiratorial grin—the grin of a man who had accepted his losses and was pressing forward regardless. He did not know that those losses had a source. He did not know that a man had looked at his family and calculated exactly how much ruin would be useful. He would go to Nice believing his misfortunes were the product of bad luck and his own poor judgment, and she would let him believe it—because telling him the truth was not justice. It was simply a different kind of wound.

Her father chuckled and nodded toward the doorway. "Ah, the Williams family. And I believe Charles is looking your way."

Cecilia followed his gaze, her mood lifting slightly as she spotted Charles Williams weaving through the crowd with his usual easy grace. He was always a welcome distraction.

"Lady Cecilia," he greeted, bowing slightly, his charming smile bright as ever. "You're a sight for sore eyes."

"Charles, it's wonderful to see you," Cecilia replied with genuine warmth. "Is Catherine here?"

"She is," Charles said, glancing toward the doorway. "She and Mother are speaking with Lady Vincent, but she'll escape soon enough."

Cecilia's gaze flicked to Lady Vincent, who now greeted the Williams family with a warmth that bordered on maternal. It was jarring, given her usual imperious demeanor. Shaking off the unwelcome thought, Cecilia turned back to Charles.

"You always know how to brighten a room," she said, slipping her hand into the crook of his arm.

"It's a gift," he teased. "Mother says I should use it sparingly. Keeps me unpredictable."

They laughed as Catherine approached, her face lighting up when she saw Cecilia.

"I was hoping I'd find you," Catherine said, taking Cecilia's hands in hers. "I've missed you."

"I've missed you, too," Cecilia replied warmly. "How are you? India feels like it's a world away."

"I'm well," Catherine said, though her smile faltered. "But it seems we'll be staying in England for good. My grandfather's health has taken a turn for the worse. The doctors don't believe he'll survive the winter."

Cecilia's heart tightened. "I'm so sorry to hear that."

Catherine sighed, glancing toward her brother. "Father has already resigned his commission and sent for our belongings. He'll be assuming the earldom once..." She hesitated, her voice softening. "Once the inevitable happens. We'll be moving permanently to London."

"That's quite a change."

"Yes. I'll miss India—parts of it, at least—but it's nice to have the family together again. With Charles at Oxford, I hardly ever saw him."

Charles joined them with a raised brow. "What's this about me?"

"Only that you've abandoned me to Mother," Catherine teased.

Charles smirked. "A noble sacrifice. Someone had to take the brunt of her scolding."

Their lighthearted banter eased the tension that had been weighing on Cecilia's chest. As they were called to dinner, Charles offered her his arm, and she allowed herself to be swept along, if only to avoid looking at Devin.

The dining room shimmered with candlelight, the long table adorned with holly and ivy. Charles proved to be a charming companion, his easy conversation keeping Cecilia distracted from the sight of Devin seated beside Miss Glassford. Lady Vincent's approving gaze lingered on the pair, her smugness impossible to miss.

Cecilia resisted the urge to glare at them. Instead, she focused on Charles's lively anecdotes, though her attention wavered whenever Devin scratched his nose or adjusted his collar. Foolish gestures, but they sent her thoughts spinning. Was he trying to signal her? Or was she reading too much into meaningless movements?

Her gaze moved along the table to Lady Judith. She sat beside her husband, her expression composed, her attention drifting with practiced ease between the conversation at her end of the table and the pair across from her—Devin and Miss Glassford—in a way that looked casual, but wasn't. She was watching. Calculating, perhaps, or simply hoping. Cecilia studied her face for some sign of what she knew, what she suspected, what she intended. She found nothing she could read with certainty.

She glanced at Mr. Glassford. His face told her even less. He ate steadily, said little, and did not look her way once. He had agreed to stand down—and apparently he meant it. Whatever Lady Judith was doing, she was doing it without his active participation. Whether that meant he had told her of their agreement, or simply that he was too careful to involve himself further, Cecilia could not say.

When the last plates were cleared, her father stood and tapped his glass for attention. "If I may," he began, his voice steady but commanding. "I have an announcement."

The room fell silent, and Cecilia's pulse quickened. This was the plan he'd hinted at earlier, though she had no idea what to expect.

"This will be our last Christmas together here," her father said with a calm smile.

The room erupted in murmurs. Lady Vincent's expression

froze in incredulous surprise, her gaze darting to her husband as if for confirmation. "What are you saying?" she demanded. "Surely you aren't leaving England?"

"Indeed, we are," her father replied. "Lady Babbage's health requires a warmer climate. We'll be relocating to the Mediterranean coast. Nice, to be precise."

A red-faced Lord Vincent tugged at his collar. "What are you on about, Babbage?"

"My concern is for Lady Babbage. The doctor recommends sunshine and fresh air. We'll divest ourselves of all our English properties and purchase a new home there."

Cecilia's heart dropped. "Leave England?" she blurted. "Papa, you can't be serious."

Her father turned to her, his expression softening. "Cecilia, you've seen how the winters affect your mother. The doctor is quite clear—this is what's best for her."

"When?" The word came out sharper than she intended.

"Next fall, at the latest." he said firmly. "I've made up my mind."

Cecilia sat back, the weight of his words sinking in. Across the table, Devin's gaze locked with hers, his expression unreadable but tinged with something that made her chest tighten. Lady Vincent, meanwhile, looked thoroughly displeased, her lips pressed into a thin, severe line.

As the room buzzed with murmurs, Cecilia felt her world tilting, the ground beneath her shifting in ways she wasn't ready to face.

❄ 14 ❄

Cecilia

When Lady Vincent led the ladies out of the dining room after dinner, Cecilia followed in a daze.

What had her father been thinking with his plan to uproot their lives and move to Nice? Nothing there would be familiar—not the language, the customs, or the people. Announcing it publicly before even mentioning it to her or Evangeline felt like a betrayal. The decision wasn't just unexpected; it had struck like a blow, leaving her unmoored, adrift without direction.

And worst of all, moving to Nice would mean leaving Devin behind. It wasn't just the distance that frightened her; it was the thought of being separated from him before they'd had a chance to sort through the fragile, unresolved feelings between them. How could she leave him, not knowing if they could ever build a future together?

At the exit, she glanced back, hoping to catch Devin's eye. He was watching her from his seat at the dining table. Their gazes met briefly, his expression clouded with concern, but Miss Glassford crowded her forward, forcing Cecilia to move on.

In the main salon, servants had already lit all the candles on the Christmas tree, their warm glow casting flickering shadows across the room. The children would soon return from their own supper, but for now, the adults had the space to themselves.

Cecilia's thoughts churned as she stood near the tree. Her father's announcement wasn't just about moving to a new place. It was about leaving everything behind—Devin, her home, her friends, her sense of purpose. Would Mr. Glassford change his mind about their agreement? And Horace—was he truly safe? She tried to hide the worry twisting in her chest.

Lady Judith materialized at her elbow with quiet efficiency that was startling to behold.

"Lady Cecilia." Her smile was warm, her tone measured. "What a remarkable evening. Your father's announcement was quite the surprise."

"To me as well," Cecilia said, which was true enough.

"How brave of him—and of your entire family. A new country, a new beginning." Lady Judith tilted her head slightly. "You must be very devoted to your mother."

Cecilia met her gaze. "I am." She paused, then added pleasantly, "I do hope Miss Glassford enjoys the rest of the season. She must have a great many prospects ahead of her."

Something moved behind Lady Judith's eyes—there and gone, too quick to name. "She is a charming girl," she said, after the briefest pause. "We have every confidence in her future." Her gaze moved briefly across the room—toward Devin, Cecilia thought, though she couldn't be certain—and then returned. "Well," she said, with a smile that gave nothing away, "I do hope the south of France agrees with Lady Babbage. One hears such wonderful things about the climate."

"We hope so too," Cecilia said. She watched Lady Judith's face for one moment longer. Unfortunately, she learned nothing.

Lady Judith inclined her head and drifted away as smoothly as she had arrived, leaving Cecilia with nothing she could name and nothing she could dismiss.

Apparently watching for her opening, Lady Vincent approached, her expression pensive. "Your father's announcement was quite a surprise," she said. "What on earth will you do with yourself in Nice? It's such an unconventional choice."

Cecilia smiled pleasantly. "I imagine I'll continue my work with widows and orphans," she hedged. "There's always someone in need, no matter where one goes."

"Widows and orphans," Lady Vincent repeated, her tone tightening. "Cecilia, I would think caring for your invalid mother would be more than enough for you. This work of yours—while well-meaning—is hardly practical. Surely, you understand that."

Cecilia frowned. "It was my mother who first introduced me to the aid society and encouraged me to participate."

Before Lady Vincent could respond, the gentlemen began returning to the salon. Cecilia's attention shifted as Devin entered the room, his gaze immediately seeking hers. He crossed to her in a few strides, ignoring the sharp look his mother cast him.

"Cecilia," Devin said, his tone low. "I can hardly believe your father's announcement. You seemed as shocked as I was. Did you know?" As he touched her arm, his mother's eyes locked onto the movement.

His presence brought Cecilia comfort, something she sorely needed right now. "I had no idea. My parents have complained of the winters here before, but I never thought they'd consider leaving England. Still, perhaps he's right and a fresh start will do us some good."

"Not you," Devin protested. "You can't possibly go with them."

"Don't be ridiculous, Devin," Lady Vincent interjected. "Her parents can't simply leave her behind." She patted Cecilia's arm, her touch as patronizing as her tone. "Cecilia, you need stability, not reckless whims."

Cecilia's brow furrowed. "Reckless whims? I'm not sure what you're referring to, Lady Vincent."

"Your excursions, my dear," Lady Vincent said, her tone sharpening. "I shudder to think of the risks you take, visiting those unsavory neighborhoods for your so-called charity work."

Cecilia stiffened but composed herself quickly. "Visiting widows and orphans? I'd hardly characterize those trips as reckless or risky, Lady Vincent."

"Don't be naive," Lady Vincent said with a dismissive wave. "You expose yourself to all sorts of dangers. It will only be worse in Nice—you don't even speak French, do you? I hate to imagine the sort of trouble you could find yourself in." Her gaze shifted to Devin, pointed and accusatory. "She's been indulged far too much. Her father needs to take a firm hand regarding those unsupervised outings. If not, this reckless behavior will only worsen."

Cecilia's spine stiffened at the insult. For a moment, the weight of Lady Vincent's condescension threatened to press her down, but she forced herself to rise above it. Her heart hammered with the frustration of always being underestimated, but she wouldn't let the older woman see it. Instead, she lifted her chin and met Lady Vincent's gaze head-on, her voice taking on a calm, resolute tone. "I assure you, Lady Vincent, my work is neither risky nor unsupervised. I'm always accompanied by my coachman and footman, and my mother encourages my efforts."

Lady Vincent's tone sharpened, cold and clipped, like a scalpel aiming to cut. "Then your mother is wrong as well, my dear. You're being much too reckless," she insisted, each word laced with disapproval and thinly veiled disdain.

At that moment, the children streamed into the room, their delighted gasps filling the air as they caught sight of the Christmas tree glowing with dozens of flickering candles. They rushed forward in a swirl of excitement, their chatter and laughter momentarily distracting the adults.

Evangeline slipped through the throng, her gaze sharp as she took in the tension surrounding her sister. She sidled up to Cecilia, her small hand slipping into hers, and leaned close.

"Reckless?" Cecilia's voice held steady, but her hand tightened around Evangeline's. "I fail to see how assisting those in need could ever be considered reckless."

"My sister is never reckless," Evangeline insisted.

Lady Vincent's gaze shifted downward, her expression hardening as her sharp eyes landed on Evangeline. "Children should be seen and not heard."

Evangeline tilted her head, her eyes wide with feigned innocence. "Is it rude to speak the truth? I thought it was encouraged in polite company. Have I misunderstood, Lady Vincent?"

Lady Vincent's jaw tightened as her nostrils flared, a flush creeping up her neck as she pressed her lips into a thin, angry line.

"Evangeline," Cecilia murmured, placing a steadying hand on her sister's arm. "Why don't you see if the tree needs any final touches?"

Evangeline's lips curved into a demure smile, though her eyes danced with mischief. "Of course, as long as everyone remembers their manners," she said sweetly

As soon as Evangeline left, Cecilia met Lady Vincent's gaze with a composure she refused to let crack. "You suggest I'm impulsive? Selfish?" Cecilia's voice was steady, her words deliberate. "Those are harsh accusations, Lady Vincent. Have you considered that true selfishness lies in turning away from those in need? Choosing one's own comforts while prioritizing imagined dangers over the real struggles of others is not prudence—it's a lack of charity, plain and simple."

A flicker of surprise crossed Lady Vincent's face, her lips tightening into a sharp line.

"Lady Cecilia has a kind and generous heart, something I admire greatly," Devin said, his voice breaking through the tension like a steadying hand.

Cecilia froze, her breath hitching as she turned to him. He stepped closer, his expression resolute yet calm. His words were unexpected, a quiet declaration that sent a ripple through the moment. Was he truly defending her? Against his mother?

Lady Vincent's face turned crimson. "Of course you would admire her. You've always been too indulgent when it comes to that girl."

So, now I'm "that girl?"

Lady Vincent glared at Cecilia. "You're too much like your mother. Both of you have always been a touch too readily swayed by stories of ill fortune, especially when they're accompanied by an outstretched hand." Her gaze flashed toward Cecilia's father and swept over him with disdain. "Is it any wonder you're so quick to excuse the bad judgment of a weak-willed man?"

Cecilia's eyes widened with shock at the insult. Before she could think better of it, she surged forward and found herself inches from Lady Vincent. Her voice, though steady, carried a sharp edge. "Excuse me, Lady Vincent, but I think I must have misheard you. I did, didn't I? Because you couldn't possibly have been speaking ill of a guest in your home, could you? You couldn't have spoken disrespectfully of someone I hold dear."

Lady Vincent lifted her chin, looking down her nose with cold disdain. "Lady Cecilia, you should carefully consider your words right now. You don't want to say something you'll regret."

"Just as you considered your words?"

The tension between them hung heavy, sharp as a blade.

Devin placed his palm on Cecilia's back, just above her waist. She tensed at the contact, unsure if he was trying to lend her strength or silence her voice.

He looked directly at his mother, his tone firm. "I'm certain she didn't mean to offend you. You didn't, did you, Mother?"

Lady Vincent's jaw tensed as she locked eyes with Devin, their shared stubbornness sparking like flint and steel. The intensity of the moment drew a few lingering glances from nearby guests. Though most still clustered near the glowing Christmas tree, the growing hush in their corner of the room hinted that others had begun to sense the brewing conflict.

Neither Devin nor his mother seemed inclined to back down, and the clash between them threatened to escalate beyond repair. With so many lingering gazes on them, no one would emerge victorious. Everyone here would bear the fallout.

Cecilia had to intervene before the moment fractured entirely —but how?

"Enough," she said, her voice cutting through the rising tension like a knife. She turned to Lady Vincent, her tone cool but measured. "Lady Vincent, perhaps we could start this conversation over. It is Christmas, after all, and you've graciously invited us into your home. Let's not let this evening be overshadowed by harsh words."

Devin's hand brushed lightly against her back, his silent support steadying her. She met his gaze and silently urged him to yield, to help diffuse the situation. After a moment, he nodded, the hard edge in his expression softening.

Lady Vincent drew herself up, her lips pressed into a thin line. After a long pause, she inclined her head. "Perhaps you're right. But this is not over. Devin, we'll speak later."

Evangeline sidled closer, her triumphant grin returning. "Well, that was a Christmas miracle."

Cecilia gave her sister's hand a squeeze, grateful for her unwavering support. "Let's hope we don't need another."

15

DEVIN

Devin's frustration with his mother roiled within him, barely kept in check. Backing down now was one of the most difficult things he'd ever done, but he couldn't let the moment spiral further.

He flipped his hand over and firmly took hold of Cecilia's. Her touch grounded him, reminding him of what truly mattered.

Her.

It was time. Past time.

"Cecilia Paring," he said in a strong, clear voice that carried to every corner of the drawing room. "I've known you all your life. You've been a part of my world for as long as I can remember—and the longer I've known you, the more certain I've become." He paused. "Even when I was too stubborn to say so. Even when I tried to shut you out for a time so I could immerse myself in my work, you were still there—in everything I was working toward. Everything I have done to speed my way down the path to becoming a barrister, I've done with you in mind."

Had Cecilia stopped breathing? She stood statue still.

"It took me a while to realize that you cared for me too, but you left so many clues that I finally figured it out. You pushed me into the pond. You pinned flowers to my shirt hem while I napped in the old apple tree. You trained your hunting falcon to drop dead field mice on my head." He grinned, and Lord Babbage chuckled. "Most people might have found those to be odd ways of showing that you cared for me, but they revealed how you felt—and how closely you paid attention. You pushed me in the pond because you knew I wanted to swim and had been forbidden to do so. You pinned the flowers to my shirttail because I admired the crown of flowers you'd braided for yourself. At the time, I'd said that I'd look like an ass in them—even though I wanted one for myself."

She grinned at that memory.

"And you dropped dead field mice on my head so I could feed them to my pet snake. No one knew me as well as you did. No one else noticed me the way you did. No one else read my every thought and desire. And no one else ever will."

She inhaled sharply, and a single tear slid down her cheek. "Devin..."

"Cecilia, I ask you now, will you agree to be my wife?"

Devin's heart clenched. Had this been a mistake? Had he pushed her too hard, too fast? Had she expected him to wait longer, even after her father's announcement?

Devin took in his mother's infuriated expression and quickly glanced away.

"It's about bloody time," Lord Babbage said from across the room, breaking the silence.

Devin had to agree with him on that point.

Miss Glassford's muffled sob drew his attention as she rushed out of the room, Lady Judith trailing behind her.

"How dare you!" His mother whirled on him. "Your father and I made our expectations regarding your marriage quite clear."

Devin's jaw tightened. "Infinitely clear," he said, still focused on Cecilia.

"And you defy us? You know what this means. We're through with you," Lady Vincent snapped.

Cecilia gasped. "Lady Vincent, no! You can't mean that."

His mother turned on her with blazing eyes. "This is all your fault. You and your dreadful family! You're like the story of the ant and the grasshoppers. You play all summer long while others toil away."

Cecilia straightened, meeting Lady Vincent's fury with quiet resolve. "Are you suggesting that *you* toil away while I play? You, who sits in the comfort of your estate, refusing to involve yourself in our community beyond hosting lavish parties? You, who has never once lifted a hand to help those in need?" Her voice sharpened. "Your accusation is not only unfounded, Lady Vincent—it's absurd."

Lady Vincent's face darkened. "Your constant giving has left your father nearly destitute. You've thrown away your future, and I won't let you throw away our family's money as well."

"She's right on that point," Lord Babbage interjected, his tone calm but firm. "Cecilia has never been careless with my money."

Lady Vincent's glare swung to him, her loathing plain.

Horace stepped forward, placing a steadying arm around his mother. "Let's retire to discuss this privately," he said.

She hesitated, her lips pressed into a thin line, before giving a curt nod. "Now. This can't wait."

Devin extended his arm to Cecilia, and she took it, her trembling hand betraying the strength in her voice. Together, they followed Horace, Lady Vincent, and Lord Babbage out the door.

By the time Devin reached the library, Mother had already informed Father of his marriage proposal. He looked unhappy, but not at all surprised.

"Devin, I'm disappointed to hear you've behaved so rashly," his father began, his tone heavy with reproach. "But I suppose I should have expected this. You've always had a stubborn streak in you. I knew it would be your downfall one day."

Devin squared his shoulders, his grip on Cecilia's hand tightening. "I couldn't do as you asked," he said, his voice firm but controlled. "I'm sorry, but it was simply too much. I refuse to win your approval by turning my back on Cecilia. Your price is too high."

"You refuse your family?" his mother asked, her voice rising, her fury barely contained. Her glare shifted between Devin and Cecilia, her composure unraveling like a thread pulled too tight. "After everything we've done for you, this is how you repay us? You're selfish to the end." Her words cut sharply, and she shot Cecilia a contemptuous glare.

Cecilia inhaled sharply, the insult stinging, but when Devin squeezed her hand, she held her tongue. Her silence felt like a small victory, a refusal to give Lady Vincent the satisfaction of seeing her react.

"Although I understand your point of view," Devin said, his tone carefully measured, "I don't agree with it. I have to live my life to my satisfaction, not yours. The strife between you and Cecilia's family pains me, and I wish it didn't exist, but it does. Sadly, if you persist in your opposition to my marriage, I'll have no choice but to sever all contact with you. I love Cecilia and have done so for as long as I can remember."

Beside him, Horace nodded approvingly. Cecilia gasped softly, swaying slightly as the weight of Devin's declaration settled over her. A moment later, she steadied herself and gazed up at him, her expression radiant with gratitude and love.

"I don't know why this tension exists between you and Lord Babbage's family," Devin continued, his gaze shifting to his father and brother, searching for support. "But it has to end." He took in the tableau before him. His father stared down at his crossed hands, avoiding eye contact. Horace looked as bewildered as Devin felt, and Lord Babbage seemed unwilling to glance at Mother, whose face flamed scarlet under Devin's scrutiny.

"It can't end." Lady Vincent's voice trembled, and when she

finally spoke, the words were laced with a bitterness that startled him. "There's too much at stake."

Cecilia's brow furrowed, confusion shadowing her features. "What do you mean? What's at stake?"

Lady Vincent turned to Cecilia, her expression a mix of anger and anguish. "Your family has already cost me more than you'll ever know. I refuse to lose anything else."

Cecilia's mouth fell open. Judging by her expression, she seemed to read something in Lady Vincent's words that escaped Devin entirely. Her gaze darted to her father. "Papa?" she asked, her voice soft but insistent.

Lord Babbage's face hardened. "Not now," he said gruffly, his glance meeting hers briefly before sliding away.

Mother's composure shattered. Her eyes filled with tears, and with a choked sob, she turned and fled the room.

"Secrets," Horace said, his voice sharp as his gaze followed her retreating figure. He turned to Devin, his expression troubled. "That's what this is about, isn't it? Something none of us know."

Devin opened his mouth to respond, but Horace had already started toward the door. "I'll get to the bottom of this," he muttered, his steps brisk as he followed their mother.

Father rose from his chair, his face taut with barely restrained fury. He cast a scathing glare at Lord Babbage. "This is far from over," he said, his voice low and dangerous, before stalking out of the room.

That left Devin, Cecilia, and Lord Babbage staring blankly at one another. Lord Babbage heaved a sigh, breaking the silence. He fixed his gaze on Devin, his voice heavy with resignation. "Your mother and I have some history between us."

Devin blinked, the words hitting him like a physical blow. He opened his mouth to speak, but no sound came. His chest tightened as a dozen fragmented thoughts collided. "What are you saying?"

"I'd once hoped we would marry, but it didn't happen. She

chose your father. I was a younger son, and she believed she could do better."

Devin stumbled back a step, his breath catching in his throat. The ground felt unsteady beneath him, as though the foundation of his understanding about his family had shifted. "Were you in love with her?" he asked, his voice low and uncertain.

Lord Babbage shrugged, his expression wistful. "At one time, yes." He sighed deeply, the weight of old regrets etched into his features. "I left England shortly after your parents announced their engagement and took a grand tour of Europe. I was gone for nearly two years. It would have been longer, but my older brother died, and I inherited his title."

He paused, his eyes distant, and Devin's thoughts raced, trying to reconcile this revelation with the parents he thought he knew. The image of his mother—so unyielding, so commanding —was suddenly at odds with the woman Lord Babbage described. It left a sour taste in his mouth, a hollow ache in his chest.

"Once I was back, I kept to London as much as possible to avoid seeing her. That was the best decision I ever made, because that's where I met Constance. Everything changed for me after that." His lips curved in a faint smile as he glanced at Cecilia. "Your mother is the light of my life. Once I was safely and happily married, I thought all the tension between our families would disappear. I was wrong."

"What happened?" Devin asked, his voice sharper now, almost demanding. He needed answers, needed something to make sense of this tangled mess.

Lord Babbage hesitated, his brow furrowing as though sorting through memories. "After your mother married your father, I felt the constant strain in our acquaintanceship, but we eventually reached a state of equilibrium. My marriage changed all that. Your mother didn't approve of Constance and made it clear she thought her too soft and weak. Over time, I've come to believe she didn't like being displaced in my affections. I was like a toy she'd lost interest in until someone else wanted it."

Devin felt a surge of anger rise in his chest, his hands clenching at his sides. The idea of his mother treating people—treating Cecilia's family—like pawns in some unspoken game churned his stomach. "She couldn't have—" But the words faltered on his lips. He thought of her sharp words, her unrelenting judgment. Perhaps she could have.

Cecilia staggered back a step, her face pale. She turned to her father, her voice trembling. "I don't understand. Why did we come here every Christmas? Why all the garden parties? The games of lawn tennis and croquet?"

He sighed, his shoulders drooping under the weight of the past. "Because we chose to keep our private concerns just that—private. How would it have looked if we'd avoided socializing? This is a small community. Refusing to see one another would have made our problems public."

Devin frowned, a deep furrow forming between his brows. "Problems?"

Lord Babbage shrugged, his weariness evident. "There was nothing specific. Just our general disapproval of one another's choices. Your father knew of our prior courtship, and that caused some tension. Constance knows what Lady Vincent once was to me, and that knowledge has caused her pain as well. Perhaps I should have explained this to Cecilia before today, but I never dreamed that an abandoned love affair from thirty years ago could cause you pain. It appears I was wrong. Suspicion and jealousy are insidious afflictions."

Cecilia's voice was barely audible. "Was there something to be jealous of?"

He hesitated, his expression shadowed with regret. "Perhaps after she first rejected me—but that's why I went to Europe. I needed to purge her from my system." His lips quirked in a bittersweet smile. "It worked. The trip changed me. Broadened my understanding. When I look back now, I see that she and I would have been miserable together. Constance and I are perfectly suited. I'd do anything for her—including moving to Nice."

Devin exhaled shakily, his mind swimming with questions he wasn't sure he wanted the answers to. His mother's motivations, her choices—they felt like shadows now, obscured and murky, casting doubts over everything he thought he knew. He glanced at Cecilia, her face tight with the same turmoil he felt, and silently vowed that their future wouldn't be weighed down by the ghosts of the past.

Lord Babbage turned to the study's entrance, his hand resting on the doorknob. With a pointed look at his daughter, he added, "Cecilia, I think the gentleman asked you a question. I suggest you answer him."

When he left, the door clicked softly shut behind him.

Devin turned to face Cecilia, his expression solemn but his heart pounding in his chest. "I'll ask it again. Will you marry me?"

She hesitated, her gaze searching his, before asking softly, "Will your parents cut you off if I say yes?"

"Immediately." The word came out sharper than he intended, and he took a steadying breath. "They've been hinting at it for years, but today is the first day they've openly threatened it. If they don't cut me off for marrying you, they'll do it for something else." He ran a hand through his hair, the weight of years of pressure pressing down on him. "That's partly why I've pushed myself to become a barrister so quickly—so I can have my independence. Don't let their threats sway you." His voice softened, almost pleading. "Please don't."

Her eyes shimmered with uncertainty. "I don't want to be the reason you split from your family."

Devin stepped closer, his jaw tightening as he fought to hold back the frustration and longing that threatened to overwhelm him. "You aren't," he said, his tone firm but laced with a hint of desperation. "It's inevitable. You have to see that. This isn't about you—it's about them and their inability to let go."

Cecilia hesitated, her emotions a storm of love and fear, her lips parting as though she wanted to say something more. Finally, she nodded, her voice steady despite the tears glistening in her eyes. "Yes."

"Yes?" Devin asked, his breath catching as hope and relief collided within him.

"Yes," she said again, her smile breaking through the tension. "I'll marry you."

Devin's chest swelled with an overwhelming mixture of joy and gratitude. He let out a shaky laugh, his grin wide and unstoppable, and pulled her into his arms. Holding her tightly against him, he whispered, "You've made me the happiest man alive."

16

Cecilia

When dawn broke on Christmas Day, most of the guests were still abed. Only the youngest among them woke early.

Now, servants moved around the house tending to fires and emptying chamber pots, delivering water to bedrooms and setting up breakfast.

Cecilia could hear the patter of small footsteps scurrying down the hallway outside her door, along with snatches of children's whispered conversations, as well as the occasional, "Mama, is it time yet?"

Cecilia stayed warm and cozy beneath the covers. She recalled being cold during the night, but now a warm body tucked against her. She rolled over to find Evangeline there, still asleep. It wasn't unusual for her sister to creep into bed with her. She'd been doing it since they were little. After the stress of the day, Cecilia had fallen asleep early. Apparently, Evangeline had managed not to wake her when she came in.

The sound of wheels on gravel drew her attention to the window. She slid out from under the covers, careful not to wake

Evangeline, and peered through the frosted glass into the grey morning below.

The Glassfords' glossy, new carriage stood at the front of the house, luggage already strapped to the roof. Two footmen moved efficiently between the door and the boot. As Cecilia watched, Mr. Glassford descended the front steps, his coat collar turned up against the cold. He moved directly for the carriage without looking around.

Lady Judith followed, Miss Glassford on her arm. Miss Glassford's face was turned away—toward the grounds, toward the bare winter trees—her back stiff..

Cecilia watched until the carriage disappeared around the bend in the drive.

Boxing Day. He had said they would leave on Boxing Day.

Apparently they'd decided to leave even sooner.

She stood at the window a moment longer, her breath fogging the glass. She thought of her father's hollowed-out expression when he'd received the news the Mediterranean Mercantile had folded. The staff let go one by one. The house going cold. The careful silences at table. She thought of Horace, cheerful Horace, who would ride out this morning without knowing how close he had come to something she could not quite bring herself to name. Last night, when Devin had asked her to be his wife in front of the entire room, the Glassfords' scheme had collapsed more thoroughly than anything she could have engineered herself. Miss Glassford would never be the future Countess of Vincent. Horace's future was safe.

Lady Vincent would never know either. Never realize how close she had come to losing her eldest son and heir while she was busy managing seating arrangements and scheming over whist.

"Never," Cecilia said quietly to no one.

Then she climbed back into bed next to her sister, her cold feet brushing Evangeline's bare legs.

Evangeline's eyes popped open. "Merry Christmas!" She sat up straight in bed, pulling the warm covers off Cecilia.

"Did you have to sit up like that? I'm cold!" Cecilia grumbled, pulling the covers back up to her chin.

"Get up," Evangeline demanded, yanking the quilt down again. "Let's go eat breakfast."

"So early?" Cecilia tried to burrow into the lingering warmth one more time, but Evangeline wouldn't let her. Cecilia heaved a sigh of exasperation. "Are you certain someone didn't exchange my sister for some changeling during the night? You *never* want to wake up this early."

"Don't be a goose. It's Christmas. The best day of the year."

Cecilia chuckled. "It will still be Christmas in an hour."

Evangeline leaped out of bed and started searching through the wardrobe for her gown. "If you wait too long, you'll miss out on the best part of the day. I love seeing the morning unfold. The groggy adults will try to calm their overexcited children as Lady Vincent glares at them disapprovingly. It's fun to watch that old harridan transform during the day as everyone compliments her on her beautiful tree and her beautiful home and her perfect servants and her ideal gifts. I know she'll go back to being her grumpy self by tomorrow, but at least this year we won't be here for that part since we're going home this afternoon."

Cecilia groaned as she pulled her sister's pillow to her stomach for warmth. At least her feet were still warm under the blanket. Evangeline hadn't quite managed to drag the covers away completely. "This will be our last Christmas here. You know how much Lady Vincent disapproves of me as a wife for Devin."

Evangeline stilled. "Did you accept his proposal?"

A surge of pure joy flooded her, and an enormous grin curved her lips. "As a matter of fact, I did."

Evangeline whirled to face her and then darted across the room and jumped back onto the bed. "That's wonderful news.

Why didn't you tell me sooner? It's what you want, isn't it?" She threw her arms around Cecilia and smacked her cheek with a kiss.

"Of course it is. For as long as I can remember."

"Have you told Papa yet?"

"Devin did. After I agreed, he went to speak with him, and I came upstairs."

"Do you think Lady Vincent will accept you?"

"Never," Cecilia said crisply.

Evangeline sat back on her haunches. "All the more reason to savor today." She yanked the pillow out of Cecilia's arms and then pushed her toward the edge of the bed with her feet. "Get up, lazy. Let's go."

With a yelp and a laugh, Cecilia finally conceded defeat.

Twenty minutes later, they headed down to the breakfast room. As Evangeline had predicted, the children under ten were already up, buzzing with excitement as they darted around their parents. The Marchcomb twins were among them, barely managing to stay in their seats while their distracted mother looked on.

Cecilia spotted Devin approaching the door and left to meet him. He smiled in greeting—that particular smile, the one he reserved for her alone—and paused to greet her.

"I need to give you something," she said quietly, pulling him to one side. "Before you go in. But I want you to know, I've already dealt with it. No one is in danger."

He turned to face her, expression focused. She reached into her bodice and withdrew the two folded sheets—Voclain's letter and the unfinished draft—and held them out.

He looked at them, then at her. Then he took them and began reading.

The corridor was empty. She waited while he read, watching his face move through the stages of it—first recognition, then understanding, then something that tightened his jaw and stilled his hands on the paper.

He read the margin notes last. She knew when he reached them because his expression changed entirely.

He looked up. "You confronted Glassford."

"Yes." She paused. "Evangeline helped. But yes."

He looked at her for a long moment—the kind of look she had seen him use in the drawing room when he was deciding exactly how to respond to something that had surprised him. Then, quietly: "You did this mostly alone."

"I had his letters," she said. "And I used your name...told him you'd seen them and would investigate."

Something moved in his expression. "Without asking me."

"I did." She met his gaze steadily. "I'm sorry for that. But it seemed like the right decision at the time. And it worked."

He was silent for a moment. Then he folded the letters carefully and placed them in his inside coat pocket.

"I *will* look into it," he said. "Properly. Whatever evidence exists of the Mediterranean Mercantile, I'll find it." He paused. "But Cecilia—I don't think your father will ever see that money again. The company is dissolved. Voclain is in Paris. The legal path would be long and expensive and uncertain." His voice was gentle but direct. "I want you to know that before you hope for it."

She *had* known. She had known since the moment she read the letter and understood the careful architecture of what Glassford had done. "I know," she said. "That isn't why I showed you."

"Why then?"

She thought about it. "Because you *should* know. And because —" She stopped. "Because I didn't want to start our engagement with something I was keeping from you."

He looked at her for another long moment. Then he offered her his arm.

"Your father was right," he said, as they turned toward the breakfast room. "You are remarkable."

"Don't tell him that," she said. "He'll be insufferable."

Devin laughed, low and quiet, and they went in to breakfast together.

The breakfast room was bright with the particular chaos of Christmas morning—children already darting between chairs, the clatter of crockery, the smell of fresh bread and woodsmoke. They filled their plates at the sideboard and found seats side by side amid the cheerful noise.

Cecilia nibbled on a cold triangle of toast with orange marmalade, glancing toward the doorway. She hoped Lord and Lady Vincent would make their entrance soon—before one of the children grew truly unruly.

"I nearly forgot to tell you…I have good news," Devin said quietly, his tone warm and steady. "Your father and I finalized the details of our betrothal."

Cecilia straightened in her seat, her eyes lighting up. "That's wonderful! I knew he would."

Devin hesitated, his expression softening. "He had concerns about my mother, but I promised him she won't come between us."

"You did?" Her smile widened, a surge of pride rushing through her.

He nodded. "I spoke with my parents last night as well. They've agreed not to disown me—for now."

Cecilia's smile dimmed. "For now?"

Devin sighed. "Nothing I do pleases them. I'm giving it two months before they find another reason to make threats."

She frowned, the toast suddenly dry in her mouth. Sipping her tea, she asked, "Because of our engagement?"

Devin shook his head. "No, because nothing I do ever pleases them. Their threats are becoming more frequent. It's only a matter of time."

"What will we do?" she asked, her tone steady despite the flicker of worry in her chest.

"What I've always planned to do—live off my income as a

barrister." He took a bite of his eggs, his calm demeanor reassuring.

Her lips quirked. "Then my dowry becomes all the more important."

Devin set down his fork and looked at her. "Cecilia, you know I'd marry you even if you were penniless."

Her heart swelled. "I know, but the dowry helps."

"It does," he agreed with a faint smile. "I hope to use it to purchase a home. Even if I can't, we'll manage. You need to know, though—your dowry isn't essential. You are."

A slow smile spread across her face, warmth blooming in her chest. "That's one of the sweetest things you've ever said to me."

Devin raised an eyebrow, his lips twitching with humor. "Then I need to make a marked improvement."

As Cecilia smiled, her father entered the room, his presence drawing immediate attention. He strode toward them, a rare softness in his expression. "Good morning, you two," he said, his voice calm but purposeful. "Congratulations, Cecilia, Devin. I trust this match will be as strong as the two of you are together."

His gaze lingered on Devin, a shadow of something deeper in his eyes—concern, perhaps? "Marriage is a partnership, Devin. Built on trust and honesty. Never forget that."

Devin nodded, his grip on Cecilia's hand tightening. "I won't, my lord. You have my word."

Lord Babbage smiled faintly, then turned to Cecilia. "And you, my dear, will ensure this family continues to hold its head high." He glanced toward the door. "Now, I'll leave you to your morning."

As he departed, Cecilia's thoughts lingered on his words, a sense of unease flickering at the edges of her joy.

A moment later, Lord and Lady Vincent arrived. Devin's mother entered with her usual air of poise, her gaze sweeping the room like a hawk surveying its territory. When her eyes landed on Cecilia and Devin sitting together, they paused briefly before shifting away as though the sight burned her. She studiously avoided looking their way again, and the tension in her rigid posture spoke volumes.

Cecilia's stomach tightened. Lady Vincent's avoidance felt deliberate, a pointed statement wrapped in layers of disapproval, wounded pride, and something more that Cecilia couldn't quite name. Was it jealousy? The notion felt absurd—what did Lady Vincent have to envy? And yet, Cecilia couldn't shake the thought. Perhaps Lady Vincent saw her as an interloper, someone who had stolen her son's loyalty and affection. Or perhaps she resented that Devin had chosen someone she so clearly deemed unworthy. Whatever the reason, the sting of her dismissal lingered.

Out of the corner of her eye, Cecilia noticed Douglas Marchcomb's eyes widen in alarm. The boy scampered behind a chair and crouched out of sight just as Lady Vincent approached the table. Cecilia nudged Devin gently, drawing his attention to the poor child.

"He must think she's here to ruin Christmas," she murmured, her lips twitching despite herself.

Devin leaned closer, his breath warm against her ear. "I'd nearly forgotten about him. At least our scene in the drawing room last night managed to distract my mother from seeking retribution." He caught Douglas's eye and made a subtle motion, gesturing for him to crawl beneath the table at his feet.

The boy hesitated for only a moment before darting under the tablecloth. Cecilia adjusted her skirts to help conceal him, though it proved unnecessary. Lady Vincent swept past, her gaze flicking toward Cecilia and Devin for the briefest of moments before shifting away. Her rigid shoulders and tightly pressed lips betrayed a storm brewing beneath her practiced poise, though Cecilia could only guess at its cause.

Cecilia exhaled quietly. Lady Vincent's refusal to acknowledge them was both a relief and a reminder of the gulf between them.

It wasn't just disapproval—it was a refusal to engage, a retreat into icy detachment that felt entirely personal.

Lady Vincent ate sparingly, her movements precise and controlled, before rising to lead everyone to the drawing room. Cecilia and Devin followed at a measured pace, keeping an eye on Douglas to ensure he stayed out of sight. It wasn't difficult, given Lady Vincent's continued determination to pretend they didn't exist.

As the children settled near the tree, waiting eagerly for the gifts to be distributed, Cecilia couldn't help but marvel at the spectacle. Evangeline had been right—watching the excitement unfold was a delight. For a moment, Cecilia's worries faded, replaced by the simple joy of the season.

Cecilia became so distracted by watching everyone else open gifts that when Devin handed her a small box, she simply stared at it in surprise for a moment.

"For me?"

"Who else?"

"Wait." She fumbled as she slid her hand into the pocket of her dress and extracted his gift. "For you," she said, passing it to him.

"Shall we open them together?"

She nodded, but as he lifted the small box, her fingers slowed. She wanted to watch his reaction.

He paused. "Don't look now, but I think Douglas opened his Christmas gift."

Cecilia followed his gaze. "Is that—" Cecilia craned her neck forward. "Did someone give that boy a wooden sword?" she asked incredulously.

"It would appear so," Devin said, grinning. "He seems quite pleased with it."

Douglas held his wooden blade in a perfect fencing pose and leaned forward to skewer his sister's new doll in the chest. His twin let out a shriek of anger and shoved Douglas away. She clutched her doll protectively to her chest as her brother toppled onto his bottom. He sprang immediately to his feet and brandished his weapon.

"I think he's delighted with the gift," Devin said with a wry chuckle.

"Hmm. Perhaps not what I would have chosen to give a child while visiting your mother. I foresee the confiscation of a sword in that boy's future."

Lady Vincent descended on Douglas with all the precision of a hawk spotting prey. She plucked the sword from his hands and thrust it toward his father, her voice clipped. "Please ensure this stays with you—and out of my sight—until you return home."

Devin chuckled. "I didn't know you could foretell the future."

"All I did was read your mother's thunderous expression."

Evangeline, standing beside Cecilia, leaned closer and murmured, "You'd think Lady Vincent has never seen a child play before. Perhaps I could send Douglas out with a box of hats instead—safer for everyone involved."

Cecilia suppressed a laugh, but Devin caught the mischievous glint in Evangeline's eyes. Devin chuckled. "You always find solutions in the oddest places, don't you?"

Evangeline shrugged, her eyes twinkling with mischief. "It's a habit. You'll see."

Cecilia glanced at the small box he still held. "Aren't you going to open it?"

"Impatient?" He raised an eyebrow.

"Devin. Don't be coy. Open it."

"As you wish." He flipped open the lid on the small brown velvet jewelry box.

She held her breath.

He lifted his gaze to meet hers and grinned. "Is this Iustitia?"

"The Roman goddess of justice. They're cufflinks. I thought they suited you."

He extracted one from the box and peered more closely at the tiny robed woman. "It's the perfect gift. Thank you." He glanced down at the still unopened present in her hand. "Your turn."

Her hands trembled slightly as she lifted the lid of her gift. Inside she found a silver, oval-shaped pendant etched in filigree. "It's lovely."

"Open it."

She took it from the box and fumbled with the catch. When the locket fell open, she discovered he'd already put two pen and ink drawings in it so they faced each other. She and Devin were there, staring into one another's eyes. She gave a gasp and touched his image with the tip of her finger. "Devin..." Her voice caught as she traced the delicate lines of their likenesses. "It's perfect. How did you manage this?"

"The artist was working while you trimmed the tree yesterday," Devin said, nodding toward a young man with a sketchpad near the fireplace. Even now he sat with a sketchpad on his lap, making graceful sweeping strokes.

She closed it and tightened her fist around it, then sniffled.

Devin's eyebrows drew together as he leaned down to peer into her eyes. "Are you crying? Did I do something wrong?"

She shook her head. "You did something very right. This is perfect. I'm happy to know I'll have this to look at during these next months we are forced to spend apart." She sighed. "Are you certain we should wait so long to get married?"

"I am. I want to have the freedom to devote time and energy to my new wife, and I won't be able to do that until the fall. I'm sorry I have to ask you to wait so long."

"I can manage— as long as you remember to write to me."

"I will. I promise."

EPILOGUE

Dear Reader,

I should warn you—Devin and I did not, in fact, live happily ever after. Not immediately.

There was the small matter of my mother's jewelry.

My father, in his infinite wisdom, decided that the most efficient way to fund both our dowries and our relocation to Nice was to auction off my mother's collection—publicly, glamorously, and with what I can only describe as misplaced optimism. The topaz necklace. The pearl earrings. The garnet set she wore on her wedding day. All of it, to the highest bidder.

I will not pretend I was gracious about it.

The auction was to be a triumph. It was not a triumph. Someone stole the jewels.

Devin, to his credit, did not suggest that people like me needed protecting. He did, however, suggest that we find the thief—and that I was perhaps better suited to that particular task than he was. This was either a great compliment or a strategic maneuver. Knowing Devin, it was both.

If you would like to know how it ended, I suggest you read on.

Yours,

Cecilia Paring

(Soon to be Montlake, provided we survive the next fortnight)

Ready to keep reading more by Sheridan Jeane?

Start the Secrets and Seduction series with

IT TAKES A SPY

A stolen necklace. A false suspect. A woman willing to risk everything to uncover the truth.

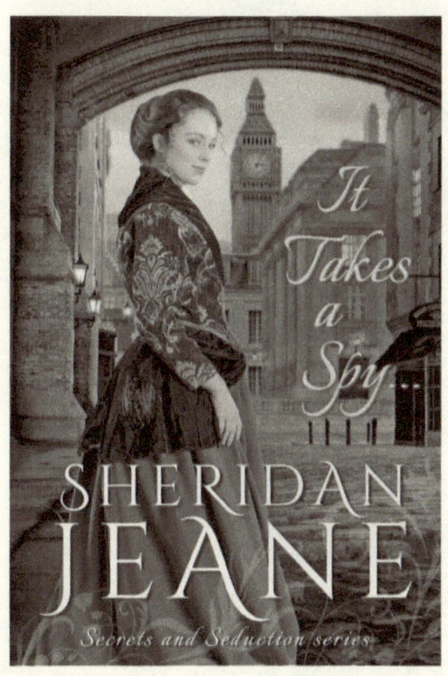

ALSO BY

Historical romances
By Sheridan Jeane
Gambling On a Scoundrel

Secrets and Seduction series:
It Takes a Spy...
Lady Catherine's Secret
Once Upon a Spy
My Lady, My Spy
Along Came a Spy
Also available:
Lady Cecilia Is Cordially Disinvited for Christmas
(only available via Sheridan's VIP club)
View the full Secrets and Seduction series and leave a review

Duke By Dawn (Novella, part of the anthology *Dukes All Night Long*)

The Shadow of the Black Rose - a Victorian-era Romantic Suspense trilogy
Whispers and Spies
The Spy In Disguise
Protect the Prince

Contemporary Romances
By Sheri Tyler
The Way to a Woman's Heart series - the **Coming Home** trilogy
Slow Simmer
Here's the Scoop
From Bitter to Sweet

The Way to a Woman's Heart series - the **Destination Wedding** trilogy
One Cup of Chemistry
Say Cheese!
Kebabs and Kisses

ACKNOWLEDGMENTS

I'm not sure why, but it took me years to decide to write Lady Cecilia and Devin Montlake's engagement story. The idea came to me in a flash one day, and I knew this was exactly the story I needed to write at that moment.

Thank you to to my son Xan for your help in plotting this book.

Thank you to Amanda Sumner for your excellent copyediting.

Thank you to Wendy LeCapra for your superb beta reading skills. Your comments and suggestions helped me make it a much better story.

Thank you to Heather Knight for your kind assistance in preparing my final books for distribution. You're a godsend and an amazingly awesome roommate when we attend conferences together.

Thank you to my good friends in the Sunshine Critique Group for your feedback regarding my book cover and to Su at Earthly Charms for creating it.

Thank you to the members of the Three Rivers Romance Writers chapter of Romance Writers of America (TRRW). The chapter's monthly meetings help keep me motivated, and you lovely writers keep me grounded.

Next to last, I want to thank Madhu Wangu. The amazing Mindful Writers groups you started in Pittsburgh have been so immensely productive for me. We go in, we meditate, then we write in silence for four hours. This is where I complete the majority of my writing.

Most of all, I want to thank you, my reader. I can't express how

much it means to me that you picked up this book and read it.
You're even reading this acknowledgement!
You're why I do this.
Thank you.

ABOUT THE AUTHOR

Sheridan Jeane grew up in Huber Heights, a suburb of Dayton, Ohio, and now lives just outside of Pittsburgh. She also writes contemporary romances under the pen name Sheri Tyler, and mystery suspense titles under S. J. Ferguson.

Sheridan has always been an avid reader and a dedicated writer. She earned a bachelor's degree in Computer Science with a minor in English.

She's thrilled to have the opportunity to share her stories with her readers. Visit her website at www.SheridanJeane.com to find ALL her books!